Galaxy Gladiators ... Series (BBW Menage)

Book Six
by Alana Khan

Axxios and Braxxus

Present Day
In space aboard the spaceship *Lazy Slacker*, formerly known
as the *Leaf on the Wind*

Chapter One

Brianna

Dr. Drayke hurries into medbay, his indigo eyes dart to the clock as if he's already stayed too long. "I came to check on Braxxus. Any changes?"

"None. His breathing is still shallow, no signs of consciousness," I say, looking over at the silver alien lying comatose in the hospital bed nearby.

The blue doctor has lost at least fifteen pounds in the last week; he tells me not to worry, it's the effect of the bonding process with his new mate. He almost died a handful of days ago because of his race's biological mating demands. I don't exactly understand the specifics, but it sounds like he and Nova have to mate several times a day or he'll get ill and possibly die.

Even though his patient is near death, the doc only breezes in for about five minutes twice a day to check on him. Otherwise, he's in his cabin with Nova. For him to have lost that much weight, they must be having sex like twenty times a day. Heck, if I'd known I could lose fifteen pounds in a week, I would have tried the sex diet, too.

"I want to thank you again, Miss Brianna. I'm sorry I've been so unavailable." The features on his handsome face have always been sharp, but with his recent weight loss, his cheekbones protrude dramatically. "This urgency to join with my new mate is bound to diminish soon."

"TMI, doc." He gives me a quizzical look; the subdural translators we all wear must have failed on that one. "Too much information," I amend.

"You Earth females are so shy about bodily functions..." he says, but he's already distracted by the information on his medpad, his finger tracing rapid patterns on the screen.

"Can you stay here for fifteen minutes?" I ask. "I just want to run to my cabin and take a shower. Seriously, I'll run. I just need a quick break—I hate to leave Braxxus alone."

His magenta lips pull down in dismay as he hails Braxxus's twin on his wrist comm. "Axxios, can you come to medbay? Don't worry, nothing's seriously wrong."

His hands are trembling so slightly a casual observer wouldn't notice, but I do.

"I'm so sorry, Brianna. I'm virtually useless at this point in the bonding process. On my planet, we take a complete lunar cycle away from our duties after our bonding ceremony. It's all I can do to be away from Nova for ten *minimas* without pain, tremors, and what she calls 'brain fog'.

"As thrilled as I am to have bonded with the woman I love, this process has taken me away from my post and put an undue burden on you. This won't last forever. I'm trying to juggle my needs with my duties. I know it's not fair that the extra responsibility has fallen to you. I apologize.

"Call me if his condition worsens. In the meantime, his brother will be here in a few *minimas* to give you a respite." With that, he dashes out of medbay.

Great. Axxios will be here in a minute. Just what I want...not.

Two months ago if I was asked if I believed in aliens and spaceships, I'd have said I only believe in hard science. That was before I was kidnapped in my sleep and taken aboard this ship as a breeding slave. That night, ten random Earth women were kidnapped and each of us was thrown into a cell with an alien gladiator slave.

I wasn't given much time to adjust to my new circumstances. Within half an hour of boarding the ship, my neck was adorned with a pain/kill collar, I was equipped with a subdural translator, and I was ordered to breed with my new cellmate—upon punishment of death. Axxios and I were forced to mate every morning in our tiny cell.

Within two weeks we overthrew our captors, and now we're fairly safe, except our former owners, the most dangerous cartel in the galaxy, are pursuing us. But right now, the MarZan crime ring isn't my biggest concern. Right this minute, the gorgeous, golden male on his way to medbay is.

Axxios. He's possibly the most handsome male I've ever laid eyes on. He's definitely the most handsome male I've ever had sex with. Sex in every possible position, at every time of day, to every level of mind-numbing bliss that could be imagined. Yeah, that male will be here in a moment, and I'll have to share this cramped ten by ten exam room with him. I'll be breathing in his delicious woodsy smell and trying to avoid the molten look of desire in his gorgeous turquoise eyes.

I consider sneaking out and running to my shower before he gets here, but I hate to leave his brother alone for even a minute—he's gravely ill. It will be so much easier on me if I don't see Axxios, though.

Against my will, my traitorous mind replays the details of what happened in our tiny cell the first time we were forced to mate. In fast forward I remember how scared out of my mind I was that first day, how unfailingly kind he was, how he made the whole enforced mating thing less horrifying than I'd ever thought possible.

Then my mind bombards me with pictures of how, despite the circumstances, the sex was life-altering. I don't know if it was our chemistry or his skill, but things happened in our little bunk I never would have believed possible. Physically, it was bliss—even under the worst circumstances imaginable.

I turn off the rolling tape of hot sex with golden boy currently looping in my head and decide to bail on Braxxus and scurry to my cabin before his brother arrives. It's too late. I hear Axxios's footsteps, then see him crash through the double doors of the medbay at a jog.

"Braxx is all right? Where's the doc? Is something wrong?" He glances at me, eyes wide in fright, then his attention flies to his twin. He slides into a chair on the other side of the bed and grabs Braxx's hand. Stroking his brother's forehead, his eyes fill with concern. A blind man at twenty paces could see how much Axxios loves his brother.

And therein lies the problem. As kind as he's been to me, as hot as the sex, as much as he wants to continue the "relationship" we have, he's never looked at me with that level of affection. And I don't want to keep having sex with him without it.

He spears me with his piercing blue gaze. "Why'd the doc call me? What's wrong?" His brows furrow in worry.

"Nothing's wrong with your brother. I need a shower, and someone has to watch Braxx. Dr. Drayke is busy with Nova and couldn't stay. I'll be back in half an hour." I bolt out the door.

Axxios

Braxx looks so frail. Looking at him used to be like looking in the mirror, only seeing my reflection in silver rather than gold. Now he's so thin, the skin on his face is tight, hugging the hollows of his bones. His muscles are distressingly slack. Gods, I couldn't bear to lose him again.

An *annum* ago we were both captains in the Mythrian fleet, doing our family proud. Ambushed by our enemy, my ship was damaged. I was taken prisoner moments after I saw my brother's ship explode. The psychic connection all Mythrian twins share was severed. All those months I assumed he was dead.

Through a lucky fluke, we found him a week ago in a slave pen on Aeon II. Beaten, abused, and with a deep stab wound in his back, he was slated for death. He'd been thrown into an outdoor stall like an animal.

I can't imagine his pain—lying there in filthy straw, soaked in his own urine, dying. When we rescued him he was covered with sores over most of his flesh, but his back was the most alarming. Dr. Drayke did everything he could despite the distraction of his bonding sickness, but Braxxus has never regained consciousness.

Not only did I think he was dead for the last *annum*, but the loss of our psychic connection has also been devastating. He and I shared it as far back as I can remember. For months after it was severed I felt a heightened sense of isolation as well as grief so crushing I thought I would die. I imagine it was the same for him.

I should feel guilty asking Brianna to be the only one on board to care for him. I know it's been a strain on her, but I trust no one else to tend him so diligently.

I smooth the silver hair off Braxx's forehead, then lean down to kiss it. My brother, my gem. The only person in this galaxy I've ever loved. A drop of liquid falls on his cheek and I realize I'm crying. I don't even want to think about the pain of losing him forever.

Brianna

I hate to interrupt him, I'm like a voyeur, standing in the doorway watching this touching scene of brotherly love. I feel so selfish, but I wish he could turn even half that much affection my way. I'd happily settle for half. Hell, I'd settle for a quarter. But I have too much self-esteem to settle for none. Which is why I can't bear to be in the same room with him. Because my body yearns for his touch, and my mind knows I can't afford to want something he can never give me.

Chapter Two

Axxios

I feel Brianna's presence before I see or hear her. My body's tuned to her frequency, like an instrument. I love my twin so much, I'm not ashamed she saw me crying over him. Perhaps she understands, although she'd never comprehend the extent of a Mythrian twin bond.

I kiss Braxx on the forehead again, then turn to face her. My cock hardens immediately; my body responds reflexively to her. She's beautiful—the sexiest female I've ever seen. I'd rut with her five times a day if I could. But she refuses.

I'd love to sheathe myself in her right this *minima*. It would turn my mind from my fears about Braxxus while giving us both pleasure. Her back is straight, her face is like stone, and she's avoiding my gaze—as usual.

"I can take it from here. I'm going to give him a sponge bath," she announces as she fills a basin with water. "Then I'll give him a massage. It's the one thing I'm competent doing; lord knows I'm no nurse," her words are light, but I can hear the tension in her voice.

It's like watching a bad play where the actors are busy doing bits of business, but their actions don't fit their emotions.

"I wish you wouldn't avoid me, Brie. I could use some comfort."

Her hands shake, and the water from the basin spills back into the sink. She makes a quarter turn so that her back is fully toward me.

"You could use some comfort? Or some sex?" She sounds hurt even though we've had this discussion and I've explained it more than once.

"Sex *is* comfort to me. And I've watched you, Brie. It is to you, too." I don't understand her resistance.

Brianna

It's hard to hide your inner feelings from a man you've opened yourself to, who's delved into your private spaces. He knows my weakness. I'd hoped he'd be consumed with his brother's health today, and just let me go about my business. But I should realize by now he's relentless.

I've never been in a real relationship before. Well, I guess I'm not in a real relationship even now.

I went from a chubby kid to a fat adolescent. I heard one of the other women on board good-naturedly refer to me as a BBW. That term doesn't really resonate with me. Especially the second "B."

Growing up overweight in America with all the size zero models and skinny actresses makes it hard to feel pretty, even if they've come up with a new, politically correct name to describe me. You can only be called names, not picked for teams in P.E., and not asked to dance at school events so many times before you get the message that you're not attractive, that you don't measure up.

I got the message loud and clear. That's why I'm not surprised Axxios doesn't want much to do with me if we're not in bed. The fact is, though, I can't bear to feel rejected— or used. Even now, I have to clench my jaw to contain the torrent of hurt, angry words that are ready to spew from my mouth.

"Lie with me, Brianna," his tone is rough with yearning, his eyes penetrating mine.

I stop pretending I'm filling this freaking basin with water and just stand facing away from him, my back ramrod straight.

"Lie with me in the other exam room. We'll hear Braxx if he stirs."

I swallow, my mouth dry with desire at the sound of his deep, persuasive voice.

I turn off the water, still presenting my back to him while avoiding the mirror in front of me. Mirrors are my enemy. I'm outflanked—enemies in front and behind me.

It's funny how I've developed the ability to look in a mirror and see only what I need to. I can notice if there's spinach in my teeth, or if my mascara ran, without seeing my double chin or plump cheeks. Right now I can avoid my own reflection even as I see his as he rises from his chair and stalks toward me.

His skin is as golden as an Egyptian statuette. His body is as muscled as a heavyweight fighter. His face is as beautiful and aristocratic as a Calvin Klein model—only more masculine. My body betrays me even as I force myself to stand straighter and avoid his image in the mirror. My nipples have already risen to firm peaks against my bra. My core is already clenching in empty need. I've lost the war before I've even waged the first battle.

"Lie with me, Brianna. Let me make you feel good." His hand touches my shoulder so lightly you'd think I could ignore it, but I can't.

"I've asked you not to do this, Axxios. I've begged you." I'm looking down at my hands in the sink, still clutching the stupid metal basin. I order myself not to glance in the mirror, his beautiful face will undo me.

His fingers slowly trace from my shoulder up to the exposed skin of my neck, then pause there, transferring their warmth to me. His hand reaches in front and grasps the vulnerable column of my neck. His touch is butterfly soft. An uninitiated observer would have no awareness of how deeply sensual this is. I imagine he can feel my carotid hammering in double time.

He bends achingly slowly, sweeping my long hair off my neck and then plants a soft, warm kiss on the delicate skin. He must know he's won when I lower my head, giving him better access to that exquisitely sensitive spot.

His lips are still pressed to my skin as he groans, "So warm, so soft, Brianna. So beautiful."

He has to feel me stiffen. He knows I hate that word. I forbade him to use it when we were locked in that tiny cell together, but he never obeyed my edict.

"So beautiful," he says again, just to assert his dominance. But at this moment I don't care. He's talking to the part of me that wants to believe his pretty lies.

His humid breath stirs the wispy hairs on my nape. He nips me there with the blunt surface of his teeth. Every nerve and synapse in my body has been flipped to on from the securely off position. At this point, we both know my agreement with his proposition is just a formality.

"Lovely Brianna. Lush Brianna. I know every delicious curve." His hands lodge at the widest point of my hips, then wend their way slowly to the indent of my waist, skim up my sides, and come to rest on my shoulders. Instead of ordering him to stop or slapping his hands away, I simply wonder when my body gave allegiance to someone else. It's certainly not obeying my orders to stand down.

"Look at us in the mirror, Brie. Look how beautiful we are together. Your lovely pale flesh contrasts against my gold. We belong together."

He has to know I won't do it. That would break the spell. With my eyes closed, I can feel attractive, if just for a moment. With my eyes closed, I can pretend I belong in the arms of this gorgeous male. The mirror, my enemy, would ruin everything. So I run away from it and turn in his arms to face him.

Tactical error! I realize immediately this position is so much more dangerous. The tips of my breasts graze his broad chest. His hard cock pulses against my abdomen. And if I open my eyes I'll be face to face with the most devastatingly gorgeous turquoise eyes I've ever seen.

"That's right," he croons. His hands span my waist and press me even closer. "Let me give you pleasure."

He bends to kiss me. His lips on mine. I still haven't said yes, although at this point we both know it's a foregone conclusion. His mouth is soft, his tongue probing. He's still in polite questing mode. The minute I give my consent, things will change. He'll unleash his full, wild sexuality on me. Every nerve in my body is on high alert, waiting for that. I know how overwhelmingly sensual that will be.

His tongue licks the seam of my lips and I open to him. My thoughts are sluggish. I'm drifting into "feel-only" mode. And yes, I'm certainly feeling. I'm aware of his warm, masculine smell, the small noises he makes from the back of his throat, and his fingers lodged in my long hair, pressing my face even closer to his.

His tongue strokes mine, gently waking up the fires inside me that I've tried to tamp down. Just these kisses, this tender invasion, the dark, spicy taste of him, the deep rumble of his moan have aroused every cell in my body.

"Let me get you naked, Brie. Let me lay you down on the bed in the next room and fulfill your body over and over again."

"Yes," I hear myself say. It's a different Brie, the damn-the-consequences Brie, the wanton Brie. I'll pay for this in an hour when she's long gone and I'm left holding the bag—the bag full of shitty feelings. But I'm powerless against his determined onslaught.

He lifts me up as if I weigh nothing and strides into the adjoining small exam room. We'll have complete privacy. Everyone knows the doctor's not here; no one will barge in.

He sits me gently on the bed, then turns away. Ever the gentleman, he rigs a blanket over the window in the door, then shuts us up in this private space.

Bending to my eye level, he stares intently at me. I know what he wants, a clear sign that my answer is yes—that I want this. I nod and Wanton Brie takes control, reaching over and slowly unzipping his blue jumpsuit, a sexy smile slashed across her brazen face.

He stands and steps out of his clothes in one lithe movement, then lifts me off the bed and onto my feet. He pulls my t-shirt over my head, then sucks in his breath as he looks at me, my breasts contained in a plain, white bra. "You take my breath away." His gaze sweeps me up and down. If the intensity of that gaze was any measure of his attraction, the gauge would be off the charts.

After sliding my leggings and panties off, he chucks them onto the chair with our other discarded clothes. He sits me on the edge of the bed and falls to his knees on the floor in front of me.

"I haven't tasted you in far too long," his voice is husky. He spreads my knees wide and licks a trail with his tongue wide and flat from my dripping core to my clit. His hands gently press me back on the bed, then lift my feet to rest on his shoulders.

"You're so open for me. Such a pretty shade of pink." He takes a deep breath in, then focuses a long, warm stream of air on my wet folds as he exhales. "I'm going to make you scream."

I have no doubt.

My clit is pulsing for him, my core is weeping for him. I don't have to wait long before he attacks with the tip of his tongue, flicking my clit, then dipping into me, then flicking again.

"Computer, lights out," I order, knowing I'll feel more comfortable in the pitch darkness.

Axxios stops the magic he's performing just long enough to say, "I've memorized how beautiful you are, Brie. Lights on or not, I can still see you in my mind's eye."

And then his tongue is back and it's relentless: teasing, suckling, thrusting. My desire is building fast; my thighs are already quivering. He sucks the mound of my clit into his mouth and applies suction while moaning in satisfaction. My first orgasm rolls through me with the velocity and force of a class 5 tornado.

"You were desperate for release," he chides, his voice deep and sexy. "I told you not to wait so long."

He says this between the soft, wet kisses he trails up my belly to the valley between my breasts. He moves onto the bed next to me now, his weight on his hip which is pressed next to mine. He bends his head close to my face.

"I'm going to play with these." He plucks both nipples in unison until I moan and writhe in pleasure. "And by the time I touch down here again," he cups my sex, "you'll be frantic for me to fill you."

Traitorous Wanton Brie leans up and kisses his soft, warm lips. My tongue penetrates his mouth as if I can't get enough of his taste—his taste mingled with mine. He leans against the headboard, his legs wide enough for me to fit between. He lays my back against his chest and his hands lavish attention on my breasts and nipples.

The feeling is intense, erotic. My head lashes back and forth against his pecs as he plays my body as if he owns it.

He stops long enough to reach down and rearrange my legs as if I'm his little doll. When he's done, my feet are close to my bottom, my knees splayed out, ensuring I'm exposed for him.

"I want you open for me, Brie. If I can't see you, I need to smell you. Now I need to hear you. I need to hear you moan."

His hands are lifting the weight of my breasts, my hard nipples spearing his palms. The intensity of my desire is so compelling I understand the term temporary insanity. Right now he could ask me for anything, he could tell me to do anything, and I would comply without a moment's hesitation.

He bends low and scrapes the tips of my nipples with his teeth. I'm on fire. I feel my next orgasm barreling down on me—I'm close.

We're both sitting up now, I'm still leaning against his chest. He's got my legs spread open, so it's within easy reach for him to place two fingers to the side of my clit and press, circling.

"Fuck," I moan low in my throat as I come so hard and so long I have time to wonder if I've ever felt such intense pleasure in all my life.

"That's right, Brie. Your body was made for this. Our bodies fit together perfectly. I'll show you."

He turns me over so I'm straddling his pelvis. I'm certain I'm painting that gorgeous golden skin with my cream. "Ride me. Take your pleasure from me." He lifts my hips and situates the blunt tip of his cock at my entrance, then takes his hands away and stills his body.

Is he doing this on purpose so I won't be able to blame him for this? So when I think back on this coupling I'll be forced to remember that I was the aggressor?

And I am the aggressor. I slide onto him in one, slow, sensual movement until he's inside of me to the hilt. I wait, with no movement, loving this moment of being completely filled, stretched, open, and invaded. And now I move. My movements are awkward at first, then I establish a rhythm and find the right angle and have another screaming whole-body orgasm. And, moments later, another.

He flips us over and begins pounding into me. His balls slap against me as his cock rams into me at a much quicker pace than I had set. I hear him panting and feel every muscle in my body tighten in anticipation.

"Now, Brie," he breathes hotly in my ear. We both launch into release at the same time. I'm aware of everything and nothing. I'm totally focused on the rhythmic contractions of my muscles as well as the shattering orgasm tearing me apart. At the same time, I could write a novel about every nuance of this golden male: the granite muscles under the velvet skin, the masculine scent of him, the sounds of our flesh touching, and of his soft grunts of pleasure.

I'd love to stop time. To stay in this moment of physical rapture, with no thinking, no nagging and scolding from the back of my mind. If I could stay in this blissful cocoon I'd live here forever.

He rolls us onto our sides, his cock still inside me. My core is still quivering in aftershocks. I realize Wanton Brie has abandoned me; it's just embarrassed, weak, lily-livered Brie who's left holding the bag.

I didn't want him to touch me for this very reason. I knew I'd hate myself when it was over. Now, with the muscles of his powerful arm loosely draped across my back, I remind myself why I'd resolved to never wind up in a bed with him again.

There's a moment in my past that I've constructed into a still photograph I carry in my head. I was at my friend Ariel's wedding reception and enjoying the toasts. There was one moment where Matt looked at her with so much love it made my stomach clench in envy. I promised myself I'd have that one day. I promised myself that someday I'd be in a relationship where my boyfriend looked at me like he loved me that much. Fat or not, I made a pact with myself that I deserved that.

And this male, whose arm is slung over my shoulder and has fallen asleep with his cock inside me, can't give me that.

Tears sting my eyes. I don't want to wake him. I don't want a scene—another scene. I just have to ensure that this, what happened in this bed just now, never ever happens again.

I'll give him one more chance. After that intense session of sex, maybe some switch magically flipped inside him. Maybe, when the lights turn on I'll see that look of love and longing on his handsome face. But if I don't, I already have a speech prepared.

Axxios

I startle awake and immediately realize where I am, and how long I've been gone from my post. I left Tyree at the helm of the ship, though he's not fully qualified; he's still in training. I should never have left him alone for so long.

"Computer, lights on dim," I whisper. I'd like to allow Brianna to keep drowsing. She's probably gotten less rest than I have over the last few days since Braxx came on board. When I'm not piloting, Tyree relieves me; at least I get decent sleep.

Brianna's been caring for Braxx day and night with no respite. *Drack*, she had to beg to get half an *hoara* off to take a shower. She's caring for him because I asked her. Perhaps I'm taking advantage. But I don't trust anyone else on board as much as I trust her, except the doc.

Gods, she's beautiful. She's female perfection, but she can't stand to even look at herself in the mirror. I wish she could see herself the way I see her. She tried to explain—said there was something in her culture that made her feel bad about herself and her body. She said Earthers don't like her form. It made no sense. I couldn't comprehend it. I can't tear my eyes from her when we're in the same room—I think she's gorgeous.

It's too bad she wants something from me I can't give. I try to understand what's missing, but her explanation never quite makes sense to me. I'd die for her, I know that.

I knew I might be killed when we overthrew the slavers who owned this ship. I was not only willing to die for my own freedom, but for her as well.

Before we launched our attack, I'd pictured the possible scenario of a laser gun pointed at her. I knew that without hesitation I'd step in front of it to protect her life. Still, she says there's something she needs from me, something I don't give her.

"I fell asleep," she says as she wipes strands of her long, brown hair off her lovely face.

"Me, too. I need to relieve Tyree. I hate to leave him at the helm for too long."

She nods, then casually commands, "Look at me a moment before you go."

I gaze into her forest-green eyes. I've been told females are inscrutable, but none more than this one. She's searching for something; I can't fathom what. I can tell by her expression she didn't find what she was looking for. Her lips quiver and her eyes brim with tears.

She's up and getting dressed in record time. She hands me my jumpsuit, it's gripped between two fingers as if she can't stand to touch anything that's been close to my flesh. She's waiting in front of the door, her back straight as a board.

"Axx, I know you love your brother," she pauses, waiting, I guess, for me to agree. I nod my head. "I've asked you to leave me alone many times since we were freed and moved to separate cabins. Yet you continue to pursue me.

"I know, I should be able to say no. I should be able to rebuff your advances. I should be able to walk away. But I'm a weak woman. So, even though this is shitty and cowardly of me, here are my terms.

"I'll continue to care for your brother to the best of my ability. As you know, I'm not a nurse, but I turn him every hour and bathe him, and I learned how to change the feeding solution in the medbot. I massage him to keep his muscles moving so they don't atrophy. I talk to him and try to let the deep part of his mind know he's safe and his brother is here waiting for him to wake up. I do all of this willingly and with a generous spirit."

"I know, Brianna. I've watched. If I haven't thanked you enough, let me thank you again. You've been more than kind." I want to please this female. I have no idea what she wants.

"You're welcome, but I need something else, Axx. If you approach me for sex again I will walk right out of medbay and never come back. I will not spend another minute caring for your brother. If you ask to lie with me, if you tell me any more pretty lies about how I look, if you even *look* at me like you want to tear my clothes off, I'm out of here. Do you understand?"

No, I don't understand. We just shared the best, most intimate sex of my life. It wasn't just me, her body spoke eloquently about her level of enjoyment. I don't understand why she wouldn't want to share that again. But by the look on her face, my time for asking questions is over.

"Yes, I understand. No sex, no asking, no looking, no...compliments. I'll stay as far from you as possible, but I will still come to visit my twin. Thank you for your help." I give her a last look, trying one more time to intuit what, exactly, she wants from me, but I get no answers. I enter the next room to press my palm to my comatose brother's cheek, then head to the bridge.

Chapter Three

Brianna

I can't imagine how that possibly could have gone worse, or how I could hate myself more than I do right now. Feeling used by a male is the worst feeling in the world.

For about half a second I allow myself to blame Axxios for everything, but I'm too honest to maintain that charade for long. I'm a grown woman. I should be able to rebuff a male's sexual advances without putting all the responsibility on him.

The last time we talked about this, I asked him directly for "more." He told me he couldn't. I didn't think he knew what love was, he led me to believe it wasn't in his culture or his biology. But now that I see him with his twin I know he's capable of love—just not with me.

There are twenty-three other souls aboard this vessel. They're all either in committed relationships or casual ones—there are no other single women. It's not like he could go online and swipe right for someone better. I'm it. I'm the only female available for a male with the libido of a well-endowed stud horse. Of course he's interested in me. Why wouldn't he be? And why not tell me I'm beautiful? Words are free.

I'm not stupid. I understand the equation: horny male + the only available female within a million miles = pretty words. Maybe I *am* stupid because I seem to fall for it every time he piles on the compliments.

Well, chickenshit way to handle it or not, he won't get near me again with his false praise. I used the right leverage—his brother.

I march to the sink and fill the basin with water; I need to take care of my "patient."

"Computer, play *Space Symphony*." It's surprising that with the music of dozens of planets in the Intergalactic Database, I've found nothing that doesn't hurt my ears. Grace, one of the women on board, composed this music since we took over the ship. Its melodic, lilting, ethereal quality usually has the ability to calm me, although I'm not sure it will work today.

I gently roll Braxx onto his back and pull his sheet down to his waist. I use the warm washcloth to clean his exposed silver skin. It's hard to believe he and Axxios are twins, even after you get past the fact that they're completely different colors.

Axx must outweigh his brother by fifty pounds. Braxx's poor nutrition not only affected his muscle tone, but he was so malnourished, there are places on his head where patches of hair have fallen out.

After cleaning his chest, I move the sheet to drape it modestly over his privates in order to get to one leg, then reverse the process for the other.

I'm not a nurse, so med-watch duty with Braxx wasn't something that came easily to me, but because I'm a massage therapist, I could do this in my sleep. I pull the sheet back up to his waist and manage to get him onto his front without rolling him off the narrow hospital bed.

His back is in terrible shape. Not only was he pierced numerous times—by swords or knives—but he's lain in his own urine for so long a great deal of his skin degraded. Dr. Drayke performed surgery on the deep gash in his back and taught me how to care for the area on a daily basis. I remove the plas-film, the clear, flexible protective layer embedded with antibiotics that covers his back. Luckily he doesn't smell like rotting flesh anymore.

I clean the area, then apply topical antibiotic and another layer of plas-film. I quickly clean the rest of him.

Now I can enjoy myself; I'm fully in my element. Back on Earth, I often used olive or coconut oil in my practice. I found some oil in the kitchen that's perfect for massage. This stuff provides just the right amount of lubrication, and it smells like fresh, clean linen.

I start on his shoulders and massage his arms and legs, avoiding any places with broken skin. While doing this, I talk to him. At first, it was awkward, but now it seems like second nature. I chatter on about my life, I ask questions expecting no answers, and I keep reminding the deepest part of his subconscious that his twin is waiting for him to wake up.

"You're getting better every day, Braxxus," I tell him cheerfully.

Despite all my efforts, it seems obvious to me that Braxxus is dying. He's been comatose since he's been on board, and he doesn't seem to be improving. Even though he's not aware of my presence on a conscious level, I believe in my heart I'm giving him comfort on a deeper level. I spend long minutes massaging every square inch of skin that isn't damaged. Perhaps my touch will wake up his muscles, or at least keep them from atrophying.

"I know you've missed your brother. Axxios is on this vessel, waiting to talk to you."

I roll him onto his back and massage his front, paying special attention to his face and scalp. When I'm done, I turn him onto his side.

"You're clean and relaxed. Now would be a great time to open those eyes and wake up."

I don't know how long he can live in this state, halfway between life and death. His body's so debilitated, and he's not getting any better.

When Axxios first asked me to sit with his brother, I had no idea I'd be alone in medbay with him indefinitely. Axx was desperate that I watch his twin, insistent that I be the first person he sees if he wakes up. I'm not sure why, but it seemed urgent and important to him, so I agreed.

I can't keep sleeping in a chair near his bedside. I don't know why I didn't deal with this days ago. After rolling in the bed from the other exam room, I slide it next to his. It smells of sex, of Axx mixed with me, so I tear off the sheets and put on clean ones.

This room is tiny. In order for me to have full access to him from one side, I have to butt the two beds together against the far wall. My mattress barely fits under the two metal medbot arms that attach to the wall. In the middle of the night, I'll have to remember they're right over my head or I'll crack my skull open. It will be worth it though, having this bed will allow me to get a decent night's sleep from now on.

I consider asking Zar, the captain, to organize a rotation of the others so they can relieve me, but discard that idea. As angry as I am at Axx, he seemed so worried about anyone other than me and Dr. Drayke caring for his precious gem; I'll hang in with my duties.

I found some ancient books from Aeon II that are pretty interesting. The translation program on the pad works fairly well. After grabbing a nutrition bar for dinner, I read for a while, then fall asleep.

The next morning I slide off the foot of the bed, fill Braxx's nutrition reservoir, and turn him over before Grace brings my breakfast. She's a pretty blonde who's always in a happy mood lately. She's Tyree's truemate now. They're such a great couple, he treats her like she's the most important thing in his world. He looks at her the way I wish Axxios would look at me. Oh well, that ship has sailed.

"Do you want me to watch him for a while Brie? You barely leave this room."

"That would be great. Did you have breakfast already?" She nods. "Mind hanging with me while I eat? Then I'll go to my cabin and be back in half an hour."

"You've been cooped up in here taking care of Braxxus for days. I'll fill you in on all the gossip while you eat, then wait for you to take a shower. No rush."

"What have we got today?" I ask, eyeing the plate she brought.

She glances at the ceiling, trying to remember the fancy name that Maddie made up for today's breakfast. "Mornu franque and blanchette creme...or is it mornu creme and blanchette franque? I can't remember. It's all still mystery food to me but I especially liked the lighter-colored stuff."

The food always tastes good. Maddie was a sous chef at Spago before she was kidnapped from Earth. And even better luck than that? She loves cooking for us. So we usually get three great meals a day, all made out of ingredients we've never encountered before. Maddie gives everything exotic names to help us enjoy it.

While I eat, Grace fills me in on how happy she and Tyree are. She informs me she's planning a talent show and wonders if I have any hidden skills.

"Not unless giving massages is considered a talent," I inform her as I take my last bite of the golden-colored mound of food that tasted a bit like curry-flavored scrambled eggs. Not my favorite thing she's prepared, but it was better than the bars we were fed when we were all captives in the belly of this ship.

When I return an hour later, I thank Grace, then turn Braxxus one more time.

I crawl back in bed and I'm half reading, half dozing when I sense something shift. I glance over and see Braxxus is awake—and staring at me. His eyes are the same gorgeous shade of turquoise as his brother's—they just look startlingly different set against his silver skin as opposed to his brother's gold.

"Angel," he croaks through a dry throat.

"You're not dead," I explain, "and I'm no angel." I scramble off the bed and get him some water. After raising the head of his bed, I hold the glass to his lips and help him drink. He doesn't take his eyes off me, even as he gulps down every drop of the water.

"Angel." He reaches out, curls a finger around a strand of my hair, and smiles. "The painting had you perfect. Down to the smallest detail." He takes a deep, calm breath, a close-lipped smile still on his face, and falls asleep.

Chapter Four

Brianna

I comm the doc and Axxios. They both make an appearance, but there's nothing for either of them to do. Dr. Drayke assures us this is great news; Braxx's vitals are stronger than they've been. I'm given the all-clear to feed him broth if he wakes again.

"I'll call you if...when he wakes again," I tell Axxios after the doctor rushes off to his new mate. "I'm sure you'd like time with him. I'll leave and you can feed him."

"I can feel the twin bond for the first time since we were separated an *annum* ago. This is a blessing." The big male is calmer than I've ever seen him. His shoulders are relaxed, and the tension in his face has softened. He must be feeling optimistic for the first time in a year.

I didn't mention the whole "angel" thing. No one really needs to know what Braxx said when he wasn't lucid.

~.~

A few hours later, I'm reading at his bedside when Braxxus opens those gorgeous baby blues again. I help him drink another glass of water, then smooth his shiny silver hair off his forehead.

He gives me a killer smile, then calls me Angel again.

"Let me call Axxios. He'll come sit with you. He'll explain everything."

"Axx is dead, too?" His smile evaporates, his forehead wrinkles as he frowns. "I'd hoped he lived."

"You're both alive. He's piloting the ship we're in. We rescued you from Aeon II. You're a free male among friends." I give him an amiable grin and comm Axxios. He'll be thrilled to talk to his brother after such a long separation.

"If I'm alive, how does that explain you?" His eyes narrow in suspicion.

"I was kidnapped from Earth. Axxios and I were prisoners together. There are twenty-four freed slaves on this ship. Plus you."

He rubs his chin with his hand and looks around the room for the first time.

"You're in medbay. You almost died. You've been in a coma for about a week." I give him an easy smile. "Looks like you're going to recover."

His brow wrinkles as he looks me up and down again. "That explains everything but you." Then his face brightens and he nods. "There are folklore tales about *ahnseek* angels. They're said to guard over those in need of assistance. You must be an *ahnseek* angel. My *ahnseek* angel." He nods calmly, happy, as if he just unlocked the secrets of the universe.

Axxios barges in and immediately notices his brother is sitting up in bed, eyes wide open. My Lord, that male looks gorgeous when his face is lit in happiness. As he rushes to Braxx's side I murmur, "I'll have someone bring broth," and leave the two brothers alone.

Axxios

Thank the Gods. Braxxus is awake. And smiling! I reach down and hug him around the neck, my cheek touching his.

"Braxx, you're going to make it." I sit down in the little chair, still warm from where Brianna sat. I clasp his hand as if I'm trying to boost our connection. I feel his emotions through our twinlink. He's confused.

"Are we dead or alive, Axx?" he frowns a bit, truly bewildered.

"Alive brother, why do you ask?"

"I...I thought I saw an angel. Our angel."

"No, you're among the living. You almost died, but you're getting better now." I'm smiling like a crazy person.

Maddie comes in to personally deliver a tray with a bowl, a spoon, and a small pot of steaming broth. "Hellooo, I'm Maddie," she says to Braxx. She always half sings her sentences; she's always happy.

"Braxxus," he says. "Salutations."

"Salutations, huh? He must be the brother who got the looks *and* the manners," she jokes. She gets serious and looks straight at him, "You're safe here, Braxxus. We all want to meet you and get to know you, but we'll give you time to get your strength back before we bombard you with good wishes.

"Promise you'll contact me if you need anything. Day or night, I'll cook you up whatever you're hungry for. We'll put some meat back on your bones."

She breezes out as quickly as she came in. I try to put a spoonful of soup in Braxx's mouth, but he's having none of that. He grabs the spoon and feeds himself.

He motions for me to pour more soup into his bowl, then asks, "Where are we, gem?" This is the name we use to refer to each other. It carries the deepest affection.

I explain that I was captured, trained as a gladiator, and was being transported on this ship to be sold. "On the way, they picked up ten Earth women as breeders—Maddie's one of them. We overthrew them and now we're on the run. As soon as you're on the mend, I'm going to ask you to give me a hand on the bridge. We need another competent pilot."

"Who's flying this craft now?"

"Tyree, but he's a trainee. We could use you."

I glance away for a moment, and when I turn back, his spoon has fallen onto the bed and he's soundly asleep.

I lower the back of his bed so it's flat and comfortable, then pull his covers up. Touching the middle of my chest with my fist, I feel the complete connection with my twin; the first time it's been at this strength in over an *annum*. I feel whole for the first time since we were separated. Now I have to figure out how to cobble the pieces of my life together and somehow find happiness.

Braxxus

I must have fallen asleep; Axx is gone. I have no idea how much time has passed, but my angel is here. I know I'll be safe.

"You tricked me for a moment, Angel. I thought I was dead. But you're a guardian angel. Thanks for your protection."

She laughs. Gods, she's even more beautiful when she's happy.

"I thought it was myth, but angels are real. And the stories about how beautiful angels are were true, too."

For some reason, she scowls at me.

"Don't worry, I haven't told anyone about you. I'll keep your secret."

"I'm not a secret, and I'm not an angel. I'm human. Just a plain old human female."

"I met Maddie. She's a human female. She's attractive in her own way, but she's not a beautiful angel like you." I wonder why she's trying to fool me. Her existence is easy enough to prove. "Axx didn't acknowledge you when he came in. That's because he didn't see you. You're an angel. *My* angel."

"Axxios certainly did see me, he was just so happy to see you that he walked by me to get to you."

"I won't argue; I don't want you to disappear. Will you stay with me until I'm well, my beautiful *ahnseek* angel?"

"You're stuck with me Braxxus. We're all stuck in this little box, hurtling through space on our way to...I don't know where. I've been tasked with watching over you, and I will do that until you're well."

"All I have to do is stay sick to keep you around?"

"I don't know about the angels on your planet, Braxx, but on my planet flirting with one wouldn't be allowed."

"So you admit you're an angel?" My voice is strong and full of energy. When she's around it's like I'm not ill at all.

"Stop it!" she scolds, but she's smiling.

Maddie comes in with another pot of soup and sets it down near my bed. "I brought bread. The doc said you could have it if you dip it in the broth. Here's a mug, it will be easier to eat that way, so no one has to feed you. Will you be okay?"

"Thanks, Maddie. I'll be fine."

"I have to run, I need to set dinner out for everyone."

"She didn't see you, either," I gloat after she leaves.

"She was just in a hurry to serve dinner to everyone else."

I shrug. "Either everyone on this vessel is being rude to you, or you're my angel. You can't fool me. I've known what you look like since we moved into the governors' mansion when we were five."

Brianna

"Governor's mansion?" This should be good. I've known his brother for several months. I'd think at some point he would have mentioned living in a *governor's mansion* FFS.

"Yes. Are you trying to trick me, Angel? You should know all of this."

"Indulge me, Braxxus."

"My fathers acted in tandem to govern one of the provinces of Mythros. They sit on the High Council of the planet as well."

"Fathers?" my voice sounds strangled even to my own ears. I shared a bed, and sex, and bodily fluids with his twin for months and this is the first mention I've heard of fathers— plural. Either he's delusional, or his brother is an even bigger ass than I'd thought.

"I'd always thought that angels, if such things were real, only attended people on my planet. I guess they do good works all over the galaxy. That would be the only reason you wouldn't know these things."

"Let's pretend I know nothing about your planet or your culture, Braxxus. Edify me."

"Mythrian males are always born twins. We're called grays until we reach puberty."

"Grays?"

"We're born that color." He points to the spoon on the bedside table. I'd call it a dull pewter.

"Go on."

"Whichever twin reaches puberty first becomes the golden one, the other turns silver. But I think you're teasing me, Angel. You have to know all of this."

"Brianna. My name's Brianna." And yeah, my tone is snippy as hell because if Axxios was here right now I'd try to freaking strangle him. Why did he never explain any of this?

I glance over at Braxxus to see his eyes wide and bright. If I didn't assume he was a hard-ass like his brother, I'd think this male was about to cry.

"What did I say?"

He's fiddling with the bedrail, frantically trying to get it down. His eyes now downcast. He finally fumbles out of bed, despite my pleas for him to stop, and gets on his knees in front of me.

"Stop it, Braxxus. Whatever is going on, stop it right now. You're going to hurt yourself. Please, stop!"

He's prostrating himself at my feet. I can't even pay attention to the fact that I'm mortified at this act, I'm so worried something is going to tear loose in his already-destroyed back.

"Get back in bed right this minute!" I use my drill sergeant voice. "Now!"

He does, then leans heavily against his pillows. He clearly over-exerted himself.

"What were you trying to do?"

"You know what I was doing," his voice is a whisper. "When an angel tells you its name, you become its servant on mortal soil. You've honored me."

"That's it!" I bark. First I motion for him to turn toward the back wall. Just as I suspected, his little slave-on-the-floor routine broke something loose. I see blood pooling underneath the clear containment of the plas-film.

I hit my comm, "Dr. Drayke, get to medbay now!" I don't care if he's balls deep in his new mate, I need him here immediately.

"Axxios, get your ass here on the double." It would serve him right if I give him a freaking heart attack because he thinks his twin is dying. Enough is enough.

If I didn't know better, I'd think Axxios teleported here because he arrives in seconds, out of breath and panicked. "What's wrong?" his voice has the shrill tone of abject fear.

"Your brother is bleeding." I see the exertion did him in and he's soundly asleep, possibly back in a coma.

"How did this happen?" His eyes are searching mine for answers.

"He was trying to worship at my feet. Somehow I think you will understand this better than I do."

He shrugs, but his eyes slide guiltily from mine.

Dr. Drayke comes in at a run, and whatever he was doing a minute ago is now on the back burner of his mind, because he's already fully in doctor mode. He gently prods Braxx's back, then grabs his pad to perform a medscan.

"What happened?"

"He got out of bed before I could stop him."

He clicks his teeth.

Fuck you, Dr. Drayke. Why am I the one to get all the responsibility and all the blame? But of course, I don't say that.

"With all that blood I thought I'd have to program the medbot to do revision surgery. But the bleeding is already slowing. I think we're good. I'll have to keep a closer eye on things."

"Good idea, Dr. Drayke. Perhaps you could check in a little more frequently," I scold him pointedly.

"You're absolutely right, Brianna. I'm going to rig a feed from the medbay computer to the one in my room. I'll stay on top of things better until the worst of the bonding urge is over."

"Not exactly what I was asking for, but I guess it will do," I don't even attempt to hide the irritation in my tone.

"I'm certain I speak for the twins as well as myself when I thank you for all your efforts." He glances at the exit as if he can't get out of here fast enough. "Feed him broth and bread as often as he'll take it. Don't hesitate to call me if there's another emergency. I'll check on him tomorrow." And....he's out the door.

Axxios

"You have some explaining to do, Axx. Don't make me pull it out of you." .

Her nostrils flare and her hands fist at her sides. I've never seen her this angry, even yesterday when she gave me that ultimatum.

I put my hands up in a self-protective motion. "Ask and I'll answer, but I don't know what's wrong."

Her green eyes are full of fire as she approaches me and pokes me in the chest with her index finger. "I'll give you hints: angels, twins, fathers, and a fucking governors' mansion."

I lean down and rub my hand over my face. "Mythrian twins have a special bond, Brianna. I've told you this before."

"Yeah, Axx. On Earth, twins have a special bond. I've heard tales that one twin will know when another twin is injured— just like you and Braxx. On. Earth. People. Don't. Have. Two. Fathers!"

"I didn't know that. You told me you had twins on Earth. I assumed things were the same with your species."

"Are you acting stupid on purpose, Axx? Why would you assume that?"

"For the same reason you assumed people only have one father, Brie."

"Don't call me Brie. I'm Brianna to you," her tone is more hurt than angry. "I'm sorry for calling you stupid, that's shitty of me."

"So you're mad I didn't mention my fathers?"

"I feel ridiculous that we spent all that time in enforced intimacy and the only thing I know about you is..." Her face burns red. She does that when she talks about sex.

"There's nothing about our chemistry we should be ashamed of Brie...anna."

"Everybody on your planet has two fathers?"

"Yes. Twins pair with one female. I believe I mentioned that if my twin were dead it would affect me in many ways. It would mean I'd never be able to have a truebond with a female."

She sits down heavily in a chair as if her legs just won't hold her anymore. Her facial muscles are slack, her eyes are closed, and tears are sliding from the corners of her eyes.

I squat next to her so I'm at eye level. I grab her hands and she makes a half-hearted attempt to pull away, but keeps them there. Being this close to her, holding her warm hands in mine, makes my cock hard. But I try to ignore it.

"When we hit puberty our bodies experience cataclysmic changes. The first of the pair to hit a certain hormonal load turns gold, the other becomes silver. But we change in other ways.

"The golden twin becomes...harder, emotionally stronger. When there's an argument we always win; we're hormonally programmed to push for what we want. Over a period of five to ten years, as we grow to adulthood, emotions disappear. That's one of the reasons the loss of my twin devastated me so badly. I hadn't had to deal with emotions of any kind for over a decade. The only true emotion we feel is toward our brother, our gem."

"So golden twins become unfeeling hardasses."

"If you want to put it that way."

"And the silver twins?"

"As they mature, they retain their emotions. I've read some books about it. It makes sense from an evolutionary perspective. There are more than two males for every Mythrian female. Long ago in our history, it became imperative that two males mate with one female. Otherwise male aggression and territoriality would have gotten out of control.

"But putting two combative males together with one female for a lifetime was a recipe for disaster. The pairing of one male with a high sex drive and few emotions with a brother capable of emotional tenderness ensures a high likelihood of happiness in a mating. "

"So, is that part of the problem with you and me, Axx? Help me understand. It takes three to...connect? You needed your brother around so you could care? About me?" She shakes her head, still confused.

"Golds don't have tender feelings. I've heard of some golds who mellow when they complete their truebond, but it's uncommon. I should have told you all of this, but it doesn't change anything. I still can't give you what you want—at least I couldn't without Braxxus."

I give her a serious look, "Mythrian females tend to be very content in their bond, Brianna. Their emotional and physical needs are fulfilled through different legs of the triad."

She gives me full eye contact, and I'm elated. I'm confident she fully understands. Perhaps if she likes Braxxus, she would consider being our bondmate. I could see that match working well for her and it would please me greatly.

"Get the fuck out." Her eyes bore into me so belligerently, if they were lasers I'd be dead.

"If you're not out in ten seconds, Axx, I'm leaving." Her jaw is so tight her lips barely moved when she spoke.

I've only hesitated half a *modicum* more when she slips one foot into a shoe.

"Okay. I'm gone," I say as I speed to beat her out the door. I may never understand Earth females. What did I say wrong?

Chapter Five

Brianna

If I wasn't so concerned about waking Braxx, I'd be kicking the metal basin around the floor like a soccer ball. I'm so angry I could spontaneously combust, and I don't know what to do with all that energy. I read somewhere you could dig your nails into a bar of soap to express your anger, but there's only a liquid soap dispenser. The same article said you could tear up a phone book; too bad those have gone the way of MySpace and the VCR.

I slip into the tiny attached bathroom, shuck my clothes, and step into a freezing cold shower. Wow! That's awful, who came up with that idea as a coping mechanism? I turn up the temp and scrub myself as hard as I can bear.

I'm so pissed I can't think. All I can do is chant, "Fuck him," over and over in my head. Ten gallons of water later, my skin is pink, bordering on red, and I've calmed down enough for other words to begin to seep into my thoughts.

Anger. Betrayal. Hurt. Confusion. Impotence.

They're all shitty feelings. I don't know which is worse. Yes, I do, actually—impotence. There's nothing I can do. Having a better understanding of why he's an asshole doesn't make him less of an asshole. And it doesn't make me better equipped to deal with his assholery.

Oh, add "bitter," to my litany of feelings. But I always come back to pissed. It's the easiest emotion to tolerate; it's motivating. I could dream up a hundred ideas for revenge. That would keep me busy and I wouldn't have to experience all those other crappy emotions.

My shower's cold now and I haven't turned down the heat. Rumor has it there's a governor on these things to keep anyone from using too much water. Water's like gold on a vessel; I knew better than to waste it.

I dress, change Braxx's bandage, feed him some soup, and watch several episodes of a shitty nature show about white bears on an ice planet, all while having a very angry conversation with Axxios in my mind. How is it that I'm conducting both sides of the conversation and I'm *still* losing?

~.~

Hours later I'm startled awake. My eyes fly open to find Braxxus staring at me with those beautiful turquoise eyes.

"You okay, Braxxus?"

"Mmm-hmmm," he nods, a serious expression on his handsome face.

He's been asleep for hours, I check his back then warm him some leftover soup.

Even though he's shoving the food in his mouth as fast as a person can without inhaling it, he hasn't taken his eyes off me.

"I'm not an angel, Braxxus. I don't even know why you think I am."

He tips the mug up and swallows the last of the broth. "I've seen your picture since I was five. I've memorized every curve of your face, the color of your hair, the arch of your eyebrow. When I was ten I took art lessons so I could draw you, then paint you. You've always been my angel—our angel." He penetrates me with a look I can't describe, like he wants to dive into me—join me under my skin.

I shake my head. "Braxxus, I still don't understand."

"Our fathers became governors when Axx and I were five. The governors' mansion was even finer than the house we grew up in; almost every room had murals on the walls and ceilings. Our bedroom was huge, and the domed ceiling was painted with angels. None were silver, gray, or gold like the Mythrian people, their skin was like yours.

"Axx and I would lie on our backs on the plush carpet and make up stories about the angels in the pictures. We created very interesting lives and relationships and heroic tales about the dozens of individuals depicted on our ceiling. And you, Br..."

He stops, eyes widening in fear, then, making a conscious effort, says my name, "Brianna, your story was always the same. You would come down from your cloud to Mythros and fall in love with us and become our bondmate. Axx and I wove many stories about you and us. We had imaginary children and hundreds of adventures together.

"There were many beautiful females on that mural, but it was never them we loved, never them we bonded with. Never them we had adventures with. It was always you."

His eyes have never left mine. He's totally sincere.

I nod while I think of a nice way to tell him how ridiculous this is. Strategy number one—don't use the word ridiculous.

"You'd never seen an Earth person before. Maybe my coloring is the same as the female in the painting. But it's not me, Braxxus. I'm just the closest person you've ever seen to what was in that painting." There, that should change his mind.

"I filled over ten sketch pads with your face. I'm intimately acquainted with the tilt of your head, the sparkle in your eye, the curve of your breast. I've been in love with you for thirty years, Brianna." He spears me with the warmest, most sincere, most heartfelt gaze one person could bestow upon another. Then he must realize the heavy import of his info dump, because his eyes slide from mine.

Holy shit, he didn't just say that. But the sincerity on his face, the timbre of his voice—he did just say it. In fact, this moment was so poignant, so deeply heartfelt, I'll be able to recite that speech, word for word fifty years from now.

"You don't know me, Braxx. You fell in love with an angel you didn't know, and trust me, I'm no angel. I'm a person, a very flawed one at that. Now that you know me, you'll figure that out real quick."

"I heard you talk to me when I was in a coma. Some of your words floated into my brain. Everything you said was kind and caring."

"Well, yeah. I'm nice—most of the time. But still, you don't know me."

"I felt your touch. You bathed me every day. Your hands were soft; your touch was tender. You cared for me without resentment."

"That's what I do...did for a living back home. It's the way I was trained."

"You can't be trained to care like that. Don't you see? It's even better if you're not an angel. You're a real female, and you were always meant for Axx and me."

I pluck the mug from his hand and set it on his bedside table, then give him a warm washcloth to clean his hands and face.

"Enough Braxx. You've tired me out. I can't argue with you for one more second." I crawl into bed and lie on my side, away from him. "Computer, lights out."

Braxxus

Maybe she's right. I guess she's not an angel. But someone painted her face on the ceiling of our bedroom. Out of all the beings depicted there, it was her face that called to Axx and me. And after Axx became golden, it was me who kept the idea of her alive. I'm the one who nurtured her memory, first in my sketchpad and then in my heart. When I lay dying on Aeon II, it was her face that haunted my dreams. It was thoughts of her that made me try to stay alive when I was ready to give up.

~.~

Axxios

Dr. Drayke told me I could bring *sumra* for Braxx's breakfast. Warm noodles in a sweet, milky sauce. It's a common dish all over the galaxy.

I've never cooked before, but I remember watching my mother in excited anticipation as she made our favorite breakfast dish. With a little help from Maddie, this tastes a lot like it came from my mother's kitchen.

My hands are full with the tray, which is heaped with tea and bread and butter and sumra; I shoulder open the medbay door.

Brianna's up, her movements brisk as she rolls Braxx onto his side and by some sleight of hand makes his bed with clean sheets with him still in it. She's bustling, her back stiff. She gives me no eye contact, nor will she look at my brother. She's upset, not just with me, but with him. I wonder what's going on, but I'm sure she'll blast me with the truth within one *minima.*

"Sumra," I announce, pretending I'm not walking into a minefield, "just like our mother used to make."

I set a huge, steaming bowl in front of Braxx. "Brianna? I think you'll like it." Smiling, I hold up a bowl toward her. It's coming, I can see by the thunderous look on her face. I hunch my shoulders as if to ward off a physical blow.

"Axxios, tell him I'm not an angel." She blasts me with a hard glare as she bundles all the dirty sheets in a pile.

"Braxx, you know she's not an angel." While her back is turned to the dirty laundry tube I give him the look I used to give him when we were kids. The look that said 'whatever you do, don't admit it to Mom.'

"I thought she was for a few *hoaras* yesterday," he says so loudly it's as if he thinks she's hard of hearing. "Now I know that's not it at all. The painting was just a sign to tell us we'd found our bondmate."

Drack. I'd cradle my head in my hands if they weren't still occupied with bowls of food. "Seriously, Braxx?" I hiss under my breath.

"Why can't we talk about it? It's got to be true—it was an omen." He looks innocent and curious, as if he was a child who just put a piece of cake in the punchbowl to see if it would float and doesn't understand why all the adults are furious.

Brianna still has her back to us, but her reflection in the mirror above the sink shows her cheeks are flaming pink like they used to be when our masters ordered us to mate.

"Braxx is obviously recuperating. Let's organize shifts for the others to watch him. I have a lot of...reading to catch up on in my room," her words are clipped; eye contact is non-existent.

"Dr. Drayke contacted me this morning, told me Braxx's vitals are strong and stable and said if it stays that way he can go to his own room tomorrow." I walk over to her and stick my face in front of hers. "One more day, Brie...anna? He hasn't been unkind, has he?"

I don't need to ask if he's been improper. I know that's not true.

"It's just so freaking awkward." She sits near his bed and grabs her bowl of *sumra.* "Delicious. You made this? I didn't take you for the domestic type." She laughs. She's sexy when she smiles.

"Braxx, do you want me to stay with you until you move to a real cabin?" she asks.

He nods. "Axx, you and I won't be together?" His brow furrows.

We've been together every night of our lives until we were assigned to captain different ships in the military. That is the way of Mythrian twins; the bond is so strong we don't do well when separated. I still don't know how our fathers pulled enough strings to get him his commission. He was as skilled as I was—he even performed slightly better than I on our exams—but he's a silver. Silvers were never given captaincies. It's believed they're constitutionally incapable of command.

"There's a large room in the abandoned wing, gem. I'll get it cleaned and we can pull two beds in there. We'll share a room again." I smile at him. I feel so lucky his life was spared and I can feel my twin connection again.

"Braxxus, I'll stay with you until you move into your cabin on one condition. No talk of angels or bondmates," she says.

"That's two conditions." He flashes her a handsome smile.

"Fine, two conditions. Can you agree to that?"

"No angels. No bondmates. No fathers. No governors' mansion. And don't call you beautiful. All the things you don't like to hear." He nods his head with finality. "As you wish."

"Are all silvers like rain-man?" she mutters under her breath, but the issue seems settled.

Chapter Six

Brianna

Braxx slept all day except when someone arrives with food. He seems to be making up for lost time and eats every bite they bring him. When he's not eating, he's sleeping, kind of like a baby—or a shark.

"Computer, dim lights." I don't want it to be completely dark in case Braxx wakes up and is disoriented. Reading isn't helping me fall asleep, so I bring out the big guns—the snow planet's white bears.

I'm awakened from a deep sleep by my awareness that there's a warm body pressed to my back and an equally warm arm slung around my waist. Possibly due to some residual caveman instinct, I freeze, ordering my brain to come fully online. At first, I'm convinced it's two months ago and it's Axx's powerful arm keeping me from falling out of the tiny bunk we shared. Then I realize the masculine arm belongs to Braxxus, which is even more distressing than the first thought.

Is he coming on to me without even asking? For a moment I thought he was the nicer of the two twins. Then I hear his deep, rhythmic breathing and realize he's sound asleep. I don't feel his engorged cock pressing against my backside; maybe he's less like his brother than I thought.

Axxios and I didn't share that tiny bunk for long, but during that time I certainly got used to having a warm front pressed against my back. It's so safe and reassuring.

As I'm debating whether or not to pull out of his embrace and possibly wake him, I'm aware the instant his consciousness shifts from asleep to awake.

"Mighty forward of you, sir," my tone is teasing and light.

His hand lifts off my body as he scoots away so swiftly I assume he'd fall off the other side of the bed if the rail wasn't up.

"Sorry, Angel. So sorry. I didn't mean to take liberties."

He's so serious—it's endearing.

"It's okay Braxxus, you were sleeping."

"You've been nothing but kind. It was totally improper of me to—"

"It's okay, really." I turn to face him. At first, I'm struck by how odd it is to see Axx's face looking out at me from silver instead of gold skin. Then I'm caught by the innocent sincerity in his blue-green eyes. "It's okay."

"I'd never want to hurt you or scare you. I just want to get to know you. I don't want to think of you as my fantasy angel anymore, I want to get to know the real Brianna."

There it is. The look. The look I would have paid my life savings, meager as it was, to receive from his brother. He's looking at me without guile. He wants nothing from me but to get to know me.

I don't know who's more dangerous, the sex god who can melt my panties with one hot gaze, or his earnest brother who clearly wants to please me in other ways.

"I'd like to get to know you, too." I smile openly at him. This twin doesn't scare me with blatant sexuality like his brother. "What do you want to know?"

"Everything. Tell me about your home planet, your mother, your fathers—your father—it's hard to think of a father in the singular," he chuckles. "Tell me about your childhood and your schooling and your work, and your...did you have bondmates back on your planet? Do you miss them?"

"No bondmates, we don't have that. One female marries one male, and I didn't have a male."

He smiles and nods, making no secret this pleases him greatly. I don't share much about my childhood, it was so mundane, but I fill him in on the life I was leading when I was kidnapped.

"You touched unclothed males for money? Did none of the males in your family object?" he asks in all sincerity.

"It's an honorable profession. It doesn't involve sexual behavior."

"Males disrobe for you and you touch their skin and that's honorable?" His brow furrows in confusion.

"Do you have female physicians on Mythros?"

He nods.

"Do they touch naked men?"

He shakes his head. "Female physicians for females, males for males."

"It's different on Earth. It's socially acceptable. You say you remember when I was touching you even though you were in a coma. That wasn't sexual, was it?"

"It would have been if I was a gold." He spears me with a sincere look.

"What?"

"If it had been Axxios instead of me, I can assure you he would have taken it as sexual."

I open my mouth to debate that statement, but then snap my mouth closed, knowing he's right. It doesn't take much for Axx to turn any situation into a sexual one.

"Well, on Earth it's an honorable profession."

He nods, "On Mythros we have *birantos*, that's honorable, too."

Do I have ESP? Because I have a sinking feeling I know where this is going. "Do tell."

"They have houses of pleasure for golds who've lost a mate or weren't lucky enough to have found one."

"You're pissing me off. Stop."

His brows rise in innocent bafflement.

"You're being obtuse on purpose. I don't touch men for money. Well, I do, but not sexually. I didn't touch you sexually. It's a completely different thing."

"I understand."

I can see by the look on his face he so totally doesn't. But at least he's smart enough to shut up.

"You've gotten your last massage from me." My lips are pursed in anger.

"I hope not, Brianna. I don't have a clear memory of exactly what you did, but what I remember was...wonderful. Maybe you'll teach me and I can massage you."

I roll my eyes. "If I didn't know better, I'd think you and Axxios were related—oh yeah, you are," I joke.

His face becomes serious. "You don't like Axx. Why?"

"I never said that."

"You didn't have to, it's obvious whenever he's in the room with you."

"You're sick, Braxxus, you've barely been awake for two minutes when Axx and I are together."

"I know what's obvious, and angels shouldn't lie."

Those gorgeous turquoise eyes seem to be looking all the way into my soul. It suddenly strikes me that Braxxus could be more of a threat than his brother. He's not only handsome, but he's capable of humor and all sorts of other, deeper emotions. I could fall for this guy, maybe I'm already tumbling for him a bit. And males from his planet don't do things solo—it's a family affair.

"I'm not lying," I lie.

He yawns and his eyes dip to half-mast.

"Get some sleep. Tomorrow's a big day, you move into your cabin."

"Mmm, perhaps you'll come with me," his words are slurring, he's exhausted.

"I already told you I'm not that kind of girl." Even as I say that a very explicit, XXX-rated picture of the three of us flashes in my mind. Maybe I *am* that kind of girl, but I'm not going to admit it.

Before I know it, his arm has snaked around my waist and his naked chest is pressed against my t-shirt covered back. His ass is jacked back away from me; there's no rapey vibe.

"Is this okay, Angel? I just want to hug you. Nothing objectionable," he adds.

I don't say anything, but it's clear I'm not objecting.

His breathing is slow and deep and rhythmic. Me? I'm wide awake. Like two 5-hour energy drinks awake. Every cell in my body is doing a happy dance. I was built to have him pressed up against me like this. Our bodies fit together perfectly. Part of me, that dirty Wanton Brie, is thinking of all the sexy things we could be doing to each other's bodies right this minute. Her core is lubricating, clutching at itself in desire.

The other me, the uptight, prudish me, feels scandalized that I'd even think such things.

"You awake Brianna? Can't sleep?" his deep voice rumbles in my ear.

"Nope."

"I upset you. I'm sorry. I know you're not a *biranto*, you're nothing like that. You're a good female. I have the utmost respect for you."

His warm breath is ruffling the hair on the top of my head. Right now I'm wishing he had a little less respect for me. I'm wondering if his lips would feel different than his brother's, if he would taste different. My heart has speeded up just thinking about kissing him.

"So what about you, Braxx? Did you have a female back on Mythros before you left for the war?"

The muscles in his arm tighten around my waist ever so slightly. I've touched a nerve. "I shouldn't have asked," I backtrack, "it's none of my business."

"That's not the way it works. Silvers don't...do that."

Uh oh. "Silvers don't do what?"

"Golds rut. Golds rut before they find their bondmate. Silvers don't."

"Pretend I don't know what you're talking about, Braxx, because I don't."

"We explained this yesterday. Golds have an overabundance of male hormones. They couldn't go without rutting until they find their bondmate. Silvers...don't."

Is he trying to confuse me?

"Silvers don't what?"

"Silvers don't have those urges."

Why is my pulse galloping in fear at this thought? Did I finally find a male who likes me only to find out he...doesn't have those urges?

And if he doesn't have those urges, why am I feeling soft, tender kisses pressed to the top of my head? And why is the arm pressed against my belly pulling me back further into his embrace?

He dips his head and whispers in my ear, "Don't worry, Brianna. Everything will work out. It always does."

Braxxus

One day ago, everyone I knew thought I was going to die. One day ago, I didn't even know I was alive. And now here I am, pressed against my bondmate. I've dreamed of her, this female, as far back as I can remember. I'm completely attracted to her, more than attracted, attached. But she doesn't know me, and really, I don't know her. And she fears me. It has something to do with Axx and she won't tell me. I wonder if <u>he</u> will.

All I know is even though my back is throbbing in pain, my body feels more alive than it ever has.

Chapter Seven

Axxios

My arms are laden with *sumra* for the three of us, as well as some fatty breakfast meat that Maddie prepared. I'll admit, I had three slices before I left the dining hall; it was delicious. I've left a dozen pieces for Braxx, it will help him put on some weight.

I shoulder my way into medbay and freeze. Braxx is lying pressed to Brianna's back, his arm around her waist. The same way I used to lie with her when we were prisoners in our cell. I'm instantly hard thinking about the incredible way it felt to sink into her plush body, even as I have a pang of...I don't know what feeling it is. I'm not supposed to have feelings. Why does my chest hurt to see my twin so close to Brianna when I'm not even allowed to call her Brie?

He thinks she's an angel...*our* angel. Of course he does, I knew he would. How could he not? She's the exact image of the angel on our ceiling. The one we fantasized about when we were kids. The one we imagined would be our bondmate. The one he sketched and painted hundreds of times. The one I've masturbated to since I got my first erection.

What if she *is* our bondmate but I've *dracked* it up beyond repair?

Brianna

Ridiculous. Why do I feel guilty that Axxios barged in and found Braxxus and me spooning in bed? Axx has no claim on me. Besides, his brother doesn't "have those urges." Crap, why does that thought make my stomach lurch?

"Breakfast," Axx announces, then distributes food to his brother and me as soon as we're sitting up. He puts a plate piled high with some gross, glistening breakfast meat patties on Braxx's lap. "Eat up, gem. You need to put on some weight."

"Are you sure these are edible?" Braxx asks as he stares at the meat, his mouth pulled down at the corners.

"Let's just say that if I wasn't concerned about putting some weight on you I would have eaten half of them in the hallway on the way here."

Braxx takes one small bite, then practically inhales the rest of the patty. "Want some, Angel?" He forks a fresh one and offers it to me.

"They look awful, I'll stick with the *sumra*. Eat fast. We've got company coming." Great timing, because at that moment Petra barges through the medbay door.

"I'm here for the hair emergency," she says with a laugh. She holds up her shears and rapidly scissors it.

I'd contacted her last night and asked her to come this morning. Braxx's shoulder-length hair fell out in patches from his malnutrition and lack of hygiene. It's as though he's been through a nuclear holocaust. It makes him look sick and pathetic.

Petra sweeps over to his bed, dumps her tools on the bedside table and focuses her total concentration on Braxx's head. "Definitely an emergency," she says as she frowns, inches her head closer to get a better look, and tousles his hair with her fingers.

Braxx is now sliding his hand through his hair. He hasn't been out of bed since he's been on board. He certainly hasn't looked in a mirror.

"I didn't know there was such a thing as a hair emergency." His eyebrows have risen high on his forehead.

"Don't worry, you're in capable hands," I reassure him.

"I've got you covered, B." Petra motions for me and Axxios to back away from the bed then grabs a clean flat sheet and ties it around Braxxus's neck to catch falling hair. "Glad you're back among the living. We were all worried about you. I'm Petra."

"Greetings and salutations." Braxxus lowers his head in an attempt at a bow.

Petra is the prettiest of all the Earth women on the ship. If there is such a thing as reincarnation, and if I could put in an order for my next body, it would be hers. She's five feet, zero inches and petite without being skinny. She's perfectly in proportion, except for her breasts which are huge on her tiny frame.

She works out a lot and does amazing gymnastic routines on a rope she's rigged to the high ceiling in the gym. Her face is pretty, although I liked her hair better when it was brown. Her long hair is dyed platinum at the moment.

I glance at Braxxus, wondering where his eyes might be focused, since Petra's giant boobs are inches from his face as she leans to get a better view of the top of his head. He's looking expectantly at her face, waiting for her pronouncement.

"I'd hoped you had enough hair to salvage so I could style what was left, but that's not gonna happen. The best I can suggest is a skull trim."

Braxx blanches and pulls back against his pillows. I have no idea how that came across in the subdural translators we all wear, but by the look on his face, I think he's imagining decapitation.

His fear isn't lost on Petra. "Don't worry, big guy. No handsome silver males will be harmed in the process of this haircut." Her laugh is deep and genuine. Having been on the same tiny ship with her for several months, I know she isn't flirting. She's in a serious relationship with Shadow.

She grabs the clippers she bought last week on Antar 7 and turns them on. Using the gizmo on the pale hairs on her arm, she shows him how it works. "I'm going to shave your hair almost to your skull, B. You're so handsome it will bring out the color in your baby blues. You ready?"

"Whatever Angel wants, as long as my head stays on my body."

Petra gives me a questioning stare. "What say you, *Angel*?" Lots of emphasis on that last word.

"I think you'd look better, Braxx. Those empty patches…" I shake my head and my nose wrinkles.

He nods at Petra and she immediately gets to work.

"I should get back to the bridge," Axxios says.

"You don't want to wait for the big unveiling?" Petra asks, never taking her eyes off her work.

"I asked Petra to come early so when she's done you could help Braxxus with a shower," I inform him.

"I'll come back later. I just hate to leave Tyree alone at the helm for too long. I'll bring lunch and help you then, gem," Axxios says, then leaves.

I guess this style isn't rocket science, because Petra's done in a few minutes.

"Oooh, you look terrific, B. Don't worry, if you hate it, it will grow out." She hands him a mirror and he nods approvingly and smiles at Petra.

"Thank you, Petra."

"See? Your head stayed on your shoulders. What do you think, *Angel*?" she asks.

I nod. "So much better than before."

"Walk me out," Petra commands as she gathers her things.

When we're outside the medbay doors she leans close and asks, "Soooo, is it A? Or B? Or A *and* B?"

"What are you talking about?"

"I've been wondering for weeks if there was trouble in paradise with you and A. Now B is calling you Angel and A looks like he's suffering from constipation. Just wondering…"

"Not A. Not B. Not A *and* B. None of the above, Petra," my tone is petulant. "We all swiped left."

"B calls you Angel and looks at you like you hung the moon. *He* didn't swipe left. Just sayin'."

"He woke up from his coma less than twenty-four hours ago."

"Yeah, but all those sponge baths…" She winks at me.

"Shadow's probably in the *ludu*s, waiting to watch your ass as you climb that rope. Thanks for cutting Braxx's hair," I say pointedly.

"They're both so handsome, Brie. Figure out who can make you happy."

"Neither," I whisper to her retreating back.

~.~

I walk in to find Braxxus running his hand over his head.

"This feels fantastic. Come touch it," he sounds five years old. "Come on!"

He's so excited. By the look on his face, I thought he didn't like his haircut. I touch his head quickly with one finger, like I'd touch a snake.

"No, like this." He grabs my hand and forces it to stroke his hair. It feels really neat, like spiky velvet.

"Cool!"

"I'm itching like crazy. Too bad Axx couldn't get me into the shower." He leans forward and scratches his neck.

"There are grab bars and a shower stool. If I could help get you there, think you could handle it on your own?"

"Yes. A shower would feel great." He smiles at me with a warm, happy gaze. A lesser male would be making references to the sponge baths I gave him. Hell, even Petra took a cheap shot at that. But Braxxus is not a lesser male.

I retrieve a towel from the attached bathroom and hand it to him. "I'm told us Earth women would be considered prudish on other planets, but I'd appreciate it if you would wrap this around your waist before we get you out of bed.

"You're not prudish, Angel, you're perfect."

Braxxus

Standing, then being helped into the shower was much harder than I thought it would be. I put more of my weight on Brie than I'd wanted to, but between leaning on her shoulder, and the rolling lab chair she brought in, we got the job done.

I'd been so happy to be alive, to be reunited with my twin, to be getting to know my angel, that I'd pushed away thoughts of what happened to me on Aeon II—and prior to that.

I don't want to dwell on the negative. As the silver, I've been the buffer for Axx's taciturn personality most of my life. I don't need to share what I suffered at the Glee'non's hands. My role has always been to be the happy one who lightens the mood. I don't complain. My struggles need to look easy. But as I sit on this little shower stool, being pelted with warm water, the torture of those dark days comes racing back.

We'd had no intel that the enemy had stealth technology—they struck out of nowhere. We were outnumbered as well as taken by surprise. Their marksmen hit with precision and struck our fuel supply; over half the ship was destroyed in one laser burst. We were dead in space, no engine or thruster power. It was child's play for them to board us, kill most of my males, and take me prisoner.

The Galaxy Standards of War Act dictates how to treat prisoners. Officers are to be kept alive if possible for humanitarian reasons. I was kept alive, but not for any lofty motives. I was kept alive to torture.

My enemies brought me back to their planet and threw me in a small cell with a few of my officers. After I tried to stage a revolt, they put us all through unspeakable physical abuse. They broke my spirit as well as my bones. One by one my men succumbed to the torture.

Every evening after the Glee'non medic came to my cell to patch me up so they could torment me the next day, I would focus my thoughts on two things: my gem and my angel. Even though I couldn't feel Axx through our twinlink, I never believed he was dead. I hung on for long days that turned into months.

Thoughts of Axxios kept me going. He and I are two halves of one soul. Mythrian twins aren't extremely close to their mother or fathers. The way we're built, we're bonded only with each other until we find our bondmate. Then instead of a dyad, we're a triad.

I endured day after day of persecution, but at some point, their medic said he couldn't keep repairing me anymore, and they lost interest in torturing me. They sold me to slavers who transported me to Aeon II for sale. I'm certain my failing health was a huge disappointment to them. They weren't going to make much money off of me. I'll have to ask Axx how much they bought me for. Perhaps the slavers gave me away to avoid the cost of incinerating my body.

I imagine the blue doctor's scans revealed the damage the enemy inflicted on my body. I hope he didn't share it with my gem. Axx spent so much of his life protecting me. What he's unaware of is I've done my fair share of protecting him in ways he'll never know. I don't want him to worry about me. It would break his heart to know how much I suffered. I'll keep up my simple, happy front. It's one way I can make his life easier.

The water turns cold, which pulls me out of my depressing thoughts. I'm alive now. I'm eating nutritious food, and soon I'll be back to my old self, only better. I've found my bondmate.

I've spent my entire life living up to the expectations of others. My fathers wanted us to go into the military, it was what the sons of highborn Governors did to prepare for politics later on.

But that wasn't what I wanted. In fact, it's hard to know what you want when you're never allowed to want it. But after a year of torture, I've had plenty of time to dream of possible futures. And the one that kept me alive was the fantasy of reuniting with my gem, of finding a bondmate who looked just like Brianna, and of having children. If I'm lucky enough to do that, I'll never try to mold them into something they aren't. I'll let them find their own way.

I've found my own path. And that path involves the beautiful female who's only a few *fiertos* away outside my door.

Brianna

"Braxx? You okay?" He's been in there long enough for the water to have turned cold. I'm starting to worry. I call again, wait a few seconds, and when he doesn't answer, I barge in. "You okay?"

I've caught him buck naked, one arm out of the shower, reaching for a towel. We both freeze—completely paralyzed. I have no idea where his eyes are focused because mine are captured by his beautiful silver skin shimmering with beads of water.

Although I'm trying desperately not to be a complete degenerate, I can't control my eyes from their slow slide down his body. He's tilted away from me, so I can't see his sexy bits. What I can see, from the hollows of his haunch to his narrow waist to his wide shoulders makes me weak in the knees.

"Sorry! So sorry! I pictured you comatose on the shower floor. My bad." I finally slam my lids shut and exit stage right.

Holy shit. Braxx's body is beautiful. Then my brain bitch-slaps me with pictures of the two of them together: Axx's thickly-muscled startling gold skin, and Braxx's thinner frame in silver. Both sets of turquoise eyes staring at me with heated desire.

"Stop it, Brie," I whisper to myself. "Stop it right now, that's enough!" I've got to get a handle on myself—or better yet, a leash. I want to run down the hall to my room so I don't have to face him. He had to have seen me perving on him. But he barely made it to the bathroom, he'll need my help getting back to bed.

Anyway, it's too late to run, I hear the door to the restroom opening.

"Hey, Angel, want to help me back in bed?" This is the first time I've heard this rough, sexy timbre to his voice. When I finally get the nerve to turn and look at him he seems different, more...direct. He's not looking at me playfully right now, not like when he ordered me to touch his velvety crew cut. No, he's looking at me like I'm a juicy steak and he's exceedingly hungry. His gaze is hot enough to melt metal.

I hurry over, slide next to him, and help him back to bed. My right arm encircles his slim, damp waist, his hand rests on my shoulder. He's trying not to put his weight on me, but with every step, he leans on me a little more. When I get him to the bed, he's panting and spent, but he's still spearing me with a look that says he wants only one thing—and that thing is me.

Situating him on the bed with one foot on the floor, I have access to his back to reapply the plas-film. I make sure he's well covered down below before I make quick work of the process.

"Lie with me, Angel." He pats the bed next to him as he lies gingerly on his back. "Talk with me. Tell me everything that makes you you." He pats the bed again, never taking his eyes off me.

"I've told you everything that's interesting." I shrug. "There's not much more to tell."

"I want to know the names of your childhood friends and the exact color of your sky on a sunny day. I want you to hum some of your favorite songs, and tell me the plot of your favorite stories. When you trust me, I want to know what made you cry in the beforetimes—before Axx and me. And some day, perhaps you'll explain why your muscles tighten when I tell you how beautiful you are."

With his turquoise gaze still penetrating mine, it's getting harder to believe he doesn't mean those words. My stomach does a happy little flip-flop and then clenches in fear. Is this really happening?

His silver hand is still patting the bed invitingly. How nice would it be to take him up on his offer and lie in bed all day swapping stories and getting to know him? Instead, for some unknown reason I say, "I need a shower."

"Perfect," he smiles broadly. "You shower, I'll nap. When you come back could you bring lunch? Enough for three?"

I'm not sure he hears my, "Certainly," as I power through the medbay doors. I'm certain he doesn't hear my mumbled, "Shit," when I'm halfway down the hallway. Oh boy, lunch with silver and gold. Awkward.

Chapter Eight

Brianna

Just as I suspected, lunch with the two of them was uncomfortable. I'm certain if Braxx wasn't around that Axxios would have nothing to do with me. But Braxx seems intent on throwing us together, like right now. Braxx asked me to help them move into their new room. It's in the abandoned wing and is almost twice the size of my cabin.

We didn't even know this hallway existed when we overthrew our slave masters two months ago. When we discovered it, we pieced together that this ship had been stolen by the criminals who kidnapped us. By the looks of it, they killed everyone on board, left everything as is, and never again opened the doors to this area of the ship.

We've had a couple work days where everyone pitched in and cleaned it up, but no one wanted to move here despite the larger digs. It felt too creepy. We threw out the junk and kept anything we thought would be useful. Grace found an instrument that sounds like the music of the Gods. I found a few pieces of art I've put on my walls. My little twelve by twelve cabin isn't nearly as sterile as it used to be.

Axx asked Steele to help him move two beds into this room. The three of us made the beds while Braxx, now clothed only in a loincloth, sat on a comfy upholstered chair. I think it's the only soft chair on the entire ship, everything else is metal and hard plastic. Steele left, and now the three of us are alone in the room. There's been another awkward silence. That seems to be the theme of the day.

"Do you have to go back to the bridge to relieve Tyree?" Braxx asks his brother.

"There's a contract waiting to be signed. We're not sure which direction to head until that happens. We're just sitting still in space; Tyree's more than capable of handling that. I've got the night off." His eyes slide to mine then scamper away. I think the unspoken message is that I can vamoose.

I rise to leave, but before I can say goodbye Braxxus announces, "Perfect. Brie told me she'd teach me how to perform a massage, but I couldn't figure out how she could show me what to do since touching my back would only bring pain. Why don't you use Axx as a model and show me what to do, Angel?"

I picture that painting, "The Scream" by Edvard Munch, wanting to clutch my hands to my cheeks and let out a long moan just like in the picture. But the only screaming I do is inside my head. "I'm tired," I hedge, "I think I'll go to sleep."

"You never go to sleep this early. You'll just be bored in your room. How am I going to learn how to give you a massage if I can't watch you do it?"

"Really, Braxx," I work my way toward the door, "I could use some alone—"

"Gem, give her a break. She's been your servant for days without a breather," Axxios interrupts.

Great. For the first time since the overthrow, Axx and I want the same thing. He wants me out of this room as much as I want to leave.

"I know there's something going on between you two," Braxx accuses, a deep furrow between his brows. "Why won't you tell me?"

"Nothing's going on!" Axx and I protest in unison.

"Good," Braxx says with finality. "Stay half an *hoara*, Angel. Show me how to do a massage. Touch him and I'll see how to do it."

Crap. Damn. Many expletives float through my head in alphabetical order ending in shit and then circling back to crap again. How do I weasel out of this when Axx and I both said we have no motive or desire to be rid of each other?

"Axx, lay on the bed on your stomach. Wait, before you do that, pull my chair closer. Then Brie can do you."

'Do you?' Does he have any idea what he's saying? Before my brain fully processes the situation, my body responds like Pavlov's dog. Sexual desire starts to spiral deep in the pit of my stomach, maybe lower.

Crap, these guys can smell female arousal. At least I know Axxios can. I picture worms writhing in a rotting carcass—a picture from some old horror movie—anything to put a lid on my rising libido.

"Braxx. Seriously, not a good idea," Axxios says, a warning tone in his deep voice.

Braxx's jaw is set as he gets up and weakly pushes his chair near the bed for a ringside seat to a show that promises to be more entertaining than Ali vs. Foreman.

Axx hurries to his side, and pulls the chair closer, then looks at me pleadingly, obviously out of good arguments.

"This won't work at all, I'm afraid," I announce in a stern voice, then raise my hands in surrender. "I need a massage table and oil."

"I had Maddie send over some oil." Braxx points to the top of his dresser. "You didn't need a special table for me." Braxx's retort was so fast if I didn't know better I'd think it was rehearsed. "We could pull the beds apart, or Axx could lie in the middle and you could...straddle him."

This male has a mean streak! He has to know he's torturing us, but he's got an innocent look on his face. I picture the twins as kids. I'm thinking Braxxus might have gotten the two out of a lot of trouble with the angelic look he's giving me now.

Okay, there's no way out of this. My thought is to power through this and get it over with in record time. Axx is wearing one of the ubiquitous blue jumpsuits they all seem to wear. At least that's better than the skimpy loincloth he wore when we were slaves.

"Um, expose yourself from the waist up and lie here." I motion to the edge of the bed near Braxx.

When he's lying down, jumpsuit not even rolled down fully to his waist, muscles stiff as a board, I bend over and halfheartedly rub his neck.

"There you go." I stand up after thirty seconds. "That's all there is to it. Those white bears on my favorite vid are calling to me. Gotta go."

"I may have been in and out of a coma, but I know you did more than that. If memory serves, you did shoulders, scalp, arms, legs, and I seem to remember some action on my butt—that felt great by the way."

My mouth is suddenly dry. This is really happening, and there's no graceful way out. I either have to fess up and admit I have bad blood with this male's brother or force my way through this massage.

I glance at the small computer screen in the corner, note the time, and promise myself I can tolerate six hundred seconds of this. After ten minutes I'm going to bolt.

I nudge Axxios's big body closer to the middle of the bed, take a deep breath, and straddle his sexy, beefy, golden ass.

I pull the top of his jumpsuit down to his waist and can't help but admire the shimmering gold of his skin. His body is perfection: wide shoulders tapering to a narrow waist—the perfect masculine "v" shape. When we used to bunk together I'd wondered if Mythrians' body temperatures ran warmer than humans; he was always like a furnace next to me. I can't help but notice the delightful feel of my hands on that expanse of toasty skin.

Axxios and I were lovers for months. My body responds to this like I'm Pavlov's dog, only it's not my mouth that's salivating, it's my core. My fingers press into the cords of his huge neck, working the muscles underneath his flesh. I move to shoulders and instinctively begin working a knot that starts in his right shoulder and ends at his scapula.

This must feel fantastic because he moans in pleasure. He must regret that noise, because every muscle in his body tightens, especially his glutes, which stiffen under my ass.

I refuse to pay attention to the sexy man lying under me, or glance over at Braxx who I'm afraid might be enjoying this way too much. I simply check the time on the clock, certain my ten minutes must be up.

Nope. Only two minutes have passed. Four hundred and eighty seconds to go. I continue to work his neck and shoulders, then move my thumbs up his spinal cord all the way to his scalp.

Sex with Axx was always so hot and fast and furious, we never actually progressed to the soft, snuggly afterglow moments where a lover would play with her partner's hair. His long golden hair is like spun silk in my hands. His breath leaves him in a heavy huff. I'm intimately acquainted with every facet of this male's arousal cycle. It usually starts with these changes in his breathing. I imagine his cock is already hard underneath him, pressed to the bed.

Shades of a few days ago where prim and proper Brie just wants to escape the room, and Wanton Brie's body wants to gallop toward the goal line. I look down and see my nipples in hard points through the fabric of my plain black t-shirt. My breath has quickened, and it's not just because I'm exerting myself. It's not my fault! I'm performing foreplay on a sex God.

I've been so consumed with giving this massage while tamping down my desire, I didn't notice that Braxx has climbed onto the bed and straddled Axx's thighs behind me. By the heat emanating off his gorgeous silver body, I'd clock his chest about two inches from my back. This is ridiculous! I need to put a stop to it.

Braxx's hand reaches out and innocently sweeps my long hair over my shoulder so he has access to my neck. Crap! Did Axxios share his secret weapon with his brother? Or did Braxxus just stumble onto one of my most vulnerable erogenous zones?

His thumbs press along my spine as he leans forward and whispers hotly in my ear. "Is this the right pressure, Angel? Too hard? Too soft?" There's that new tone to his voice, the raspy, deeper, sexy tone.

"Just right," little Goldilocks says instead of what she should be saying, which is to tell him to get his deliciously warm hands off of me. But I don't, because Wanton Brie is taking over, and sensible Brie's vocal cords are paralyzed.

I'm having trouble paying attention to two things at once. I'm still on a fool's errand, trying to massage Axx, as well as focusing ninety percent of my attention on Braxx's gentle pressure on my aching muscles.

Braxx leans down, his cheek less than an inch from mine as he observes my strong fingers.

"Show me, Angel. Show me exactly what you want."

I glance at him and my core clenches with desire. He's beautiful. For a moment I try to choose which is more appealing, silver or gold, but it's a ridiculous quest. They're both handsome males. I think if I gave the word, all our clothes would be in a pile on the floor in ten seconds and I would be the filling in a very sexy sandwich.

"Show me, Brie," Braxx prompts.

I dig my thumbs along Axx's scapula. The irony doesn't escape me that in my house growing up we used to call this area of the body "angel bones." My mom told me this is where wings would be attached if we were angels.

Braxx leans forward and puts strength into his movements. "Like this?" He bends in, his warm breath fanning my ear.

"Umm-hmm." I nod. My resolve to keep them both at bay has been decimated. My pulse is pounding in my clit. I glance at the clock. My ten minutes aren't up yet. My resolve didn't even last ten freaking minutes.

"Show me, Brie. Show me how to make your body feel good," Braxx prompts, his tone persuasive.

My thumbs move up Axx's spinal cord, then back and forth between upper back and hairline. It's so surreal to feel the same actions performed on my neck and spine at the same pace, in the same place as what I'm doing to the male underneath me.

With a mind of their own, my fingers comb through Axx's golden hair. Braxx does this to me, only slower, which ups the erotic factor by ten.

"Is this relaxing, Brie?" Braxx whispers as he plants soft kisses starting at the crown of my head, then down until his lips reach my bare neck.

His tiny kisses morph into full-lipped nips as he adores that area with his ministrations. I hear the soft, wet sounds his lips make as he pulls the tiniest bites of skin into his mouth with his nibbles.

I suck in my breath quietly, as if it's a secret that I'm fully aroused. I picture what an interloper would observe if they opened our door. They would see Brianna, her hair a brown curtain spilling over the side of her face. They'd see me sandwiched between spectacular silver and gorgeous gold.

Perhaps I am an angel. I certainly feel as if I'm in heaven. Sensible Brie has long since left the building, and Wanton Brie is allowing herself to feel the fire licking along her veins.

"That's right, Brie. Show me just where to touch." His hands skim up my sides from my waist, gently touching the outer curve of my breasts, then chastely landing in my hair again.

"Teach me," he says as his hands repeat the same movement, only this time they brush a bit more of my breasts.

My nipples are as hard as diamonds. They desperately want to be plucked.

The third time his hands sweep the outer curve of my flanks, I twist a bit to the right and his hand grazes my nipple. I can't control my sharp hiss, my quick intake of breath.

"I see, Angel," his voice is warm and tender and compassionate. His hands skim down, only the next time they slide up they're under my t-shirt. He repeats his first movements, completely avoiding my aching buds. Liquid heat pools between my thighs as I focus on my need. It takes two more complete sweeps up and down my skin before I press my nipple into his palm. Even though I'm still wearing a bra, the sheer sensuality of this moment is so overwhelming my eyes flicker closed and I pump my needy clit against Axx's hard ass.

"Your body is perfect, Angel," Braxx breathes into the shell of my ear. My channel has to be dripping wet as well as clenching in desire.

Axxios chooses this moment to flip from his front to his back. My core is now pressed directly on the ridge of his cock, which is hard as a steel rod. I open my eyes and am face to face with his gorgeous turquoise gaze. His lids are heavy, he's highly aroused—I know all his signs.

Braxx scoots closer, his pelvis presses against my ass. He's kissing and licking my neck and ears. I have goosebumps.

Why can't I have this? In less than sixty seconds all three of us could be naked. I could impale myself on Axx's cock, lean over and kiss his warm lips and give Braxx access to whatever part of me he wants. My body loves this picture— loves this whole idea. It wants to sprint toward release. It wouldn't take much to start spasming in pleasure.

Then Sensible Brie pulls the plug on this fantasy and pushes Wanton Brie out of the driver's seat. I look at Axx with all the anger and hurt I can muster. I shake my head, dislodging Braxx's lips.

I scramble off the bed, not even bothering to explain. Pulling my t-shirt down, I finger comb my hair, slide my shoes on and bolt out the door and down the hall to my room.

Axxios

The cabin is silent after Brie escapes. Silent except both Braxx and I are panting like animals after a race.

"I need to know what happened between you two," Braxx demands, sounding more like a gold than a silver. The muscles in his face are tight, his nostrils flared.

"We were forced to mate after she was abducted." I shrug.

"Tell me why she can't bear to look at you. Why she hates you."

"Females can be inscrutable, Braxx. I'm not certain. She wants something from me. She doesn't understand the way of Mythrian twins. She wants emotions I can't give."

"Did you explain that?"

"Yes. No. I don't know. I thought I did."

"Let me ask it another way, do you think she understands it?"

I don't even hesitate to answer, "No." I shake my head. "She doesn't understand it at all."

"So she doesn't understand about golds. Does she understand silvers?"

"No. I didn't even know you were alive until a handful of days ago."

"Why didn't you tell her about the angel? Why didn't you talk about your past when you were locked in a cell together?

You know she's our bondmate, Axx. How did you *drack* this up so completely?"

"This is why golds have silvers, gem. We need you. *I* need you. I don't do emotions. Except with you, Braxx. I love you. You're right, I <u>have</u> *drack*ed this up completely." I hate that I've messed this up, more for Braxx than myself. If I'm cracking apart inside over this I can only imagine how terrible he's feeling.

"We need a plan, Axx. We need a plan and we need one quick." He pointedly looks down at his loincloth and I see his erection straining against it.

"How long have you known, gem?" my tone is low and serious.

"I've known since I opened my eyes and saw her. A blind man would know. How long have I been certain? Ten *minimas*."

"You got your first erection ten *minimas* ago?" I ask. He nods. "I thought you were dead, gem. I gave up hope several lunar cycles ago. When I met Brianna it was even more bittersweet, knowing she was probably destined to be our bondmate yet we'd never have her—not together."

Golds get erections from the day we turn gold. We rut. If there are females available, we rut a lot. *Birantos* are brought from off-world to meet our needs. Golds can be insatiable—I certainly was. Golds rut as often as we want, but we never bond. We only bond when both twins meet their bondmate.

Silvers don't sexually mature like golds. They don't rut. They become truly sexual when they've met their mate. I look at Braxx's loincloth, his cock bursting to break free. Biology doesn't lie.

"Axxios?" It's Tyree's voice over the comm. "Callista just tied down contracts for two cestus fights on Galgon. "By my calculations, that's four days away. Before we take off, I'd like you to check all the coordinates."

"That's in the Procul sector, right?"

"Yes."

"Give me a few *minimas*," I tell him and sign off. "I have a plan, Braxx."

"I'm listening."

"The cestus fights in four days will hopefully net us a load of credits. I'll convince Captain Zar to take us to the nearby planet of Fairea afterward for rest and recreation. It's been a hard couple of lunar cycles for all of us, especially the females. We all deserve a break. You and I went there years ago, remember? When we were seven or eight."

Braxx nods. "Gods we had fun. That planet was a renowned tourist spot. They have some sort of festival every day of the *annum*. We watched *mronck* races and cheered. Even our fathers relaxed a little. All the people were dressed in costumes. We were grays." His voice sounds weaker when he adds, "Everything was easier then."

"This may sound crazy coming from your gold brother, but a female would find that...romantic, right?"

Braxx thinks for a moment, then nods. "Probably."

I stand up and pull on a fresh jumpsuit. "You have six days, brother. Six days to do two things. First, I want you walking the halls, maybe even lifting some light weights in the *ludus*. I want you in shape to walk the huge fairgrounds when we get to Fairea. We're going to have fun with our female. She's going to see us in a different light."

He's nodding, the corners of his mouth turning up into a smile.

"And second?"

"You've got to work on her, brother. She's got to agree to go with us—both of us."

He frowns. "I don't think that will be easy, Axx."

"You're the first silver in Mythrian history to captain a starship, gem. I have complete faith in you."

Chapter Nine

Brianna

"Wow, Savannah." I hike up the fabric on the bust of my dress so my boobs don't spill out when I take a deep breath.

Savannah is our resident U.S. Marine slash clothes horse. It's always struck me as an interesting combo, but she seems totally at home in both roles.

"You look hot, Brianna." She winks at me and fusses with the yards of billowy skirt.

"Hot? Really?" I wonder if the guys will think I'm hot, then mentally scold myself for even caring.

"Yeah." She nods.

"Both your guys will be very interested. You're all crazy about each other if your passionate looks are any indication, yet things are obviously tense between you. I just thought I'd give Mother Nature a little push. Did you know we all call you Braxxianna behind your backs?"

I give her a questioning look.

"You know, like Brangelina?"

"For fuck's sake, Savannah."

She pulls me in front of the only full-length mirror on the ship. It's in a large room in the abandoned wing. All the women are putting last-minute touches on their dresses. Evidently planet Fairea is like a Renaissance Festival back home, except it's three-hundred-sixty-five days a year—or however long their year is. It sustains the whole planet's economy.

People dress up in old-fashioned costumes. The males on our little ship just have to throw on the fancy leather gladiator kilt-like outfits they sewed for the first party we had after the overthrow. We women, however, needed to put in a lot of effort. We looked at a lot of pics on the Intergalactic Database and it seems there's a lot of leeway, especially since there are so many species involved.

We're wearing dresses that would fit in at a Ren-Fest on Earth. Lots of decolletage, wasp waists, and full skirts. We found some Mirasian silk in a crate in the hold. Evidently, it's hella expensive and quite sought after in the galaxy. Oh well, spoils of war.

As I look in the mirror, I have to say I look pretty good. I should have been born in this time period. It nicely displays my assets—boobs! The nipped-in waist gives the illusion that I have a waist, and the full skirt hides my wide hips. I twirl this way and that, actually liking what I see.

"You look great, Brie. Let me help Zoey, I think she needs alterations and we have less than two hours until we touch down."

"Brianna!" Petra calls over the din of so many conversations. "Hair and makeup over here!"

She sits me down in a hard little chair and brings out makeup and brushes.

"We were kidnapped in our p.j.'s, Petra. Where did you get the stockpile of makeup?"

"Every time we stop at a planet and they ask me to do my sexy rope routine to make money I pick up some supplies." She tilts her head and shrugs. "You have such a beautiful complexion you don't need much makeup. What hairstyle do you want?"

We do a whirlwind search on the database and decide on a French braid crown, with enough of my thick, brown hair down that some length will still flow down my back. Petra's fingers fly and we're done in minutes.

How lucky, I got hair and makeup done without any intrusive questions.

As I help a couple of other women with their dresses, I reflect on the last few days.

At first, I thought Braxx should apologize for his behavior during the massage. He orchestrated that, not Axx, and it ended so badly. I finally decided that running out of the room wasn't exactly proper adult behavior on my part either, so I quit expecting an apology.

Braxx has made it a point to eat with me every day. He's been building up his strength. He asked me to walk the halls with him. He's gotten a lot stronger, but I'm still glad Dax, the handiest guy on the ship, made him a tall wooden staff. Dax said he found the wood in one of the cargo bays. It's amazing the stuff we've found there.

B and I talked a lot about our home planets when we were walking around the ship. He's shown me pictures of his homeworld. He wasn't joking when he said he wanted to know everything about me. He actually got me to hum a couple of my favorite songs and tell a few stories. I narrated the plot of the movie *Avatar*. I thought he'd love it, but it lost something in the translation.

He asked me to go to planet Galgon with him two days ago to watch Aries and Savage's cestus matches, but I declined. I was afraid I'd see one of them get hurt. Thankfully both males won handily and came back to the *Slacker* without a scratch.

After six days of meals and walks and singing and stories, I feel comfortable with Braxx. I'm not sure how things will be with Axxios, though. I'm hoping he decides to stay on board at the helm. I even hinted that to Braxx several times today, but I don't think he took the bait.

"Females and males," Captain Zar announces over the comm. "I'm happy to tell you we've landed on Fairea. My lovely Anya tells me we're here for what she calls Rest and Relaxation. So be it. As you all know, Aries and Savage won their gladiatorial matches on Galgon and the purses were larger than expected. There are enough credits for each of you to have money to spend on your holiday. This will be dispensed to each of you as you exit the ship.

"Research shows the fair is rife with pickpockets, rigged games of chance, and some of the galaxy's lowest riff-raff. As a former slave, I don't give orders lightly, but consider it an order that none of you, male or female, travel alone on Fairea. No one. I hope I make myself clear.

"We all have bounties on our heads. If we see signs of the MarZan cartel we may need to take off in a hurry. Please stay in touch through your wrist comms and check back here every *hoara*.

"My appreciation to Dr. Drayke and Nova who have volunteered to stay on board and man the comms."

He pauses a moment. Even though he's on the bridge and we're all elsewhere in the ship, he's probably giving us a moment to chuckle. Drayke and Nova still can't go an hour without mating. It's no hardship for them to stay on board. The bridge will probably smell like sex when we return.

"So everyone be safe, have fun, and check back every *hoara*." The comm clicks off, then on again. "We leave atmo at 2105. Back on board by 2100 at the latest."

A moment later I run into A and B near the exit area. I actually get a little weak in the knees. They're standing at my door in their sexy gladiator regalia. Axxios already had a fancy uniform. He and his brother must have been sewing today because now they're both wearing the hottest black leather outfits in the entire Procul sector.

I think there are skimpy loincloths cradling the family jewels. Over that, they're wearing a thick black belt with a strip of black leather hanging down the middle from waist to knee. The strip is about four inches wide, just enough to make you wonder what it's hiding. They have black sashes from one shoulder to the other side of their waist.

Ohmygod. How can a person go from zero to one hundred on the arousal scale in one freaking second? The black leather slashing across their gold and silver skin? Ah-mazing.

But even cooler than that? The smoldering look they're giving me. Two sets of turquoise eyes are looking me up and down and up again. Maybe Savannah was right about the boobage I'm showing. My twins are certainly making these twins happy.

"Could you forgive me if just for today I use the b-word, Brianna?" Braxx asks respectfully.

My eyebrows and the corners of my mouth lower.

"Maybe other b-words then? How about breathtaking?"

"Beguiling," Axx adds.

"Bewitching," Braxx is making this a game.

"Ravishing."

"Hey, that's not a b-word," I complain.

"It is in our language," they both tell me at the same time, then laugh.

"Lovely."

"Stunning."

"Captivating."

"Tantalizing."

"Enough!" I interrupt.

They both bow low to me, then come up smiling.

"You ready?" Axx asks.

I nod. "How's your back, Braxxus. Let me see."

He turns around. His entire back is exposed in this outfit, but it's covered in plas-film. My fingers gently trace some of the worst cuts, but overall it looks much better.

Braxx turns, grabs the wooden staff he'd leaned against the wall, and takes my right hand in his left; Axx grabs my other hand.

After complimenting all the lovely ladies and alpha males queued up in the exit area, our feet touch Fairean soil. The cloudless sky is almost bottle green with its three weak suns shining down from different quadrants of the sky. I assume I'll get used to the eerie quality of the daylight by the time we leave.

I've been to the Renaissance Festival near Denver several times, and this has the same vibe, only it goes on as far as the eye can see in all directions. We get a festival map on an interactive vid card when we pay our entry fee, then move off to the side to plan our strategy.

I let the guys pour over the map as I watch the organized chaos all around me. Our intel was right, we would have felt foolish without our costumes. I even see babies in strollers who are dressed for the fair.

I've gotten off the ship on two different planets since I was abducted, so the sheer enormity of seeing dozens, maybe hundreds of different alien species isn't completely shocking. But it's still oddly compelling eye candy to see different skin colors, numbers of limbs and digits, and facial configurations.

The reptilian species, of which I've counted three already today, give me the skeeves in a deep place in the pit of my stomach. Like seeing mold growing on food, there's something in my own primitive brain that just shouts "stay away" from something with scaly skin and vertical pupils.

I smell meat cooking on an open fire and hear people hawking their wares. Music is drifting toward me from at least two directions. For the first time since leaving Earth, I hear an alien tune with a pleasing melody; my body hums with pleasure. It reminds me of the type of music I heard at the Ren-Fest back home. The melody lilting toward me from my right sounds like a flute and a stringed instrument. I want to go watch them play. In fact, I want to see everything there is to see before my feet hit the *Lazy Slacker's* ramp at 2100.

"Brianna, come give us your opinion," Braxx calls.

I approach and try to make sense of the vidscreen he hands me. They flank me and show me various exhibitions they think I'll enjoy. While I hold the screen, first a silver, and then a gold hand point out different locations on the map. They suggest a schedule and a route.

"What do you guys want to see?"

"Whatever pleases you," they say almost simultaneously.

Oh, I could get used to this—two handsome males who want to cater to my every desire. Yes, please.

"This schedule you're showing me, you'd enjoy this too, right?"

They nod.

"Then let's get a move on."

The first exhibition we'll attend sounds like an elaborate *mronck* show. They say it's dozens of six-legged horse-like animals being put through their paces while being ridden by people standing on their backs. Sounds fun.

It's in two hours, so we have plenty of time to stroll through rows and rows of outdoor stands selling arts and crafts and food.

After only ten minutes I'm almost on overload. We've seen paintings, leathercraft, beautiful dresses and shawls, interesting things made out of silky ribbons, as well as jewelry of every description. At almost every stall, Braxx finds something he thinks I'll like and shows it to me.

"Would you like this, Angel?" he shows me a gorgeous pendant of silver, gold, and rose gold intertwined. The shine and patina of both the gold and the silver closely resemble the two handsome guys standing in front of me. With a little imagination, you'd think it was a lovely symbol of the three of us.

"You have a very good eye, B, but I'm sure we can't afford that, and besides I don't need it." Even as I'm saying no, I caress it with my index finger. "It's really beautiful, though."

"Just like someone else I know," he smiles and hands it back to the shopkeeper.

He's so freaking sweet I just don't have the heart to keep scolding him about calling me beautiful. I'll let this personal battle go—for today.

As we walk from shop to shop, Axx stays close, his right hand possessively around my waist. At first, I wanted to push him away, but I have to admit I like his protectiveness. I feel safe with him. I realize I always have.

I'd expected to get a lot of judgy, disapproving looks as we walk along. Two guys escorting one girl. But this seems to be a complete non-issue. First of all, it's a time-honored part of the Mythrian culture. Second, with the sea of diverse creatures we're wading through, no one would have time to focus on something as benign as three people enjoying each other's company.

And I am. I *am* enjoying both their company.

"Axx, remember the *revensell* we had when we were here as kids? It's been almost thirty years and I can still almost taste how delicious it was," B's voice is happy and expectant.

"I do remember. Do you recall how huge it seemed? I imagine it wasn't nearly as big as I remember."

"If we see a *revensell* stand, I'm getting one, even if I'm not hungry." Braxx's eyes are shining in excitement. It tickles me the way he can be almost childlike in his enthusiasm. Then a picture of the look in his eyes the night of the massage arrows into my brain. He wasn't so childlike then. My nipples harden; I wonder if they'll show from under the silky fabric of my dress.

"Are you going to try it, Brianna?" Axx asks.

It takes me a moment to realize he's not talking about having a sweaty threesome in their big bed. "Something so delicious you're talking about it decades later? Count me in. What is it?"

"Meat on a bone roasted over a spit. It's amazing," Braxx answers. "Take a sniff, that's probably what you smell."

"But…" Axxios begins. "When we find a booth, one of us will buy it while you wait with the other."

"Sure," I shrug. "Why?"

"You…won't want to see the beast it comes off of. There will be pictures of the animal prominently displayed. You won't like them," Axx explains.

"Look at me," I motion down my body. "I am not a vegetarian. I've seen very cute pictures of all the animals I've eaten, and I've scarfed the food down anyway, much to the dismay of my vegetarian friends. But cute brown eyes or not, I love steak."

"Trust me, Angel, you won't want to see pictures of this one," Axx says, shaking his head.

Axx just called me Angel. And it made me tingle from the top of my head to the soles of my feet. Especially in the middle. My nether region just flipped the switch from off to on. I can feel my pulse drumming between my legs.

"The animal is too cute?" Frankly, I don't care. I'm just prolonging this conversation as an excuse to keep looking at him. His skin actually glistens in the sun—he's beautiful.

"The animal is not cute. Brianna. Trust me on this. You'll enjoy the *revensell* way more if you just imagine what it looks like."

His expression changes from a serious warning look to a warm smile. Axxios is smiling at me! I don't believe I've ever seen him smile like that. It makes my clit tingle. If this keeps up it's going to be a very long day.

I hadn't realized, but Braxxus had been scouting ahead. He's hustling back, barely using the wooden staff in his hand, a wide grin on his face. "Right down this aisle. The *revensell* looks great and smells fantastic. You were right, Axx, there are huge pictures of the *revens* at the front and back of the stall. I'll buy us each one and then let's check out the next aisle over."

Now they've got my interest piqued. If I don't see a picture today, I'm getting on the Intergalactic Database when I get home tonight.

Did I just call the *Lazy Slacker* home? This awareness jolts me. It's been several months since I was kidnapped from my apartment. Do I really feel like the *Slacker* is home?

I search myself for a moment. Colorado is far behind me. We've all agreed none of us Earth women can go back. At this point, we've been gone too long. There are questions we just couldn't answer. One of us would spill the beans and we'd either become lab rats at some secret, military black ops site, or we'd be locked away in the loony bin for the rest of our lives.

So if Denver isn't my home, it's clear that home is where I hang my hat. And that's the *Slacker*, with all my friends.

We're like family, a great big slightly dysfunctional family, but a family nonetheless. I know without a doubt that everyone on board cares about me and would try to protect me if I needed it.

They're all way too much in my business—just like real family. They call us Braxxianna, FFS. But they all want me to be happy. I feel peaceful inside, believing the truth of the statement that the *Slacker* is home and this is my adopted family.

I glance up at Axx, who's scanning the crowd protectively while his hand absently caresses my side from hip to below my bust.

He's not a bad male. I'm having a hard time remembering why I've been so angry at him. He's been nothing but kind. From the first moment I was thrown into his cell, he tried to calm my nerves while never being condescending or sugar-coating the truth. It's not his fault there's something in his biology that gives him macho man syndrome.

Braxxus is approaching us. In addition to his staff, he's trying to juggle three pieces of meat that look like something out of the *Flintstones*. These things are huge, like turkey legs only triple the size. Each one could feed a family of four for a week.

They both turn their attention to me as Braxxus hands me the haunch-o-brontosaurus. I'm not particularly optimistic even though it looks good and smells so delicious my mouth is watering. I probably should have just taken a look at the damn pictures in the stall. They couldn't be worse than what I'm imagining in my head.

But I bite into it and the taste is amazing. The meat is so succulent and juicy I reach for the napkin Braxx is already handing me. My mouth is full of the delectable, hot meat and all I can do is nod and make a "yum" noise.

"We told you," Axx smiles. Braxx says nothing. His mouth is so full, he's not capable of anything other than chewing.

The guys make a point of making a U-turn so we don't walk by the pictures they are convinced will offend me. If I can eat ham after seeing pictures of adorable piglets, I'm sure I'll be able to tolerate seeing a *reven*.

We explore a little shop run by a wizened old humanoid with a green cast to his leathery skin. He's making the most attractive shoes out of buttery-soft suede. I'd love a pair. We've had the damnedest time finding comfortable footwear in space, but he says he couldn't possibly get them finished before tomorrow, even after we offer him a bribe.

The guys are entranced by a huge stall that specializes in knives. There are knives of every shape, size, and description from every planet in the known galaxy. It's interesting for a minute, but by now I'm bored out of my mind.

"Guys, I know we're not supposed to separate, but can I go look at the next couple of shops?" I lean closer and whisper, "I'll scream if I need help. Promise."

Axx's eyes slit suspiciously. "No, Angel, I'll go with you."

"That's sweet, but you're fascinated here. Look," I point, "I won't go farther than that tree. Just a few shops up the path."

When neither of them agrees, I offer, "I'll stay in the middle of the path so you can see me at a glance."

That seems to do the trick, and off I go. The next shop holds no interest for me. It's run by an exotic female selling potions. She has almost snow-white skin and green lips. She tries to get me to come closer so she can rub something into my palm, but I have a good excuse not to get lured in.

The next stall isn't a stall at all. Toward the back of the space, there's a rope hung between two trees about four feet off the ground. A multi-colored blanket is slung over the top of the rope, creating a triangular shelter like an old-fashioned pup tent.

But it's not the tent that catches my attention, it's the animal? Male? Being? Sitting to the side of it.

He's definitely male. I know this because he's wearing no clothes, not even a scrap of loincloth. His genitals are hanging out on display. He's squatting, knees splayed wide, hands on the ground in front of him in a decidedly canine posture. His body seems otherwise humanoid.

He has pointed dog-like ears, mostly hidden by his unkempt black-and-brown brindle hair. He has one ice-blue eye, one deep brown. His face has canine aspects in a way I can't quantify because what I'm really aware of is the fact that his entire attention—his entire being—is focused on the huge haunch of meat clutched in my hand.

I glance over at the guys and see that Axx is watching me like a hawk. I salute him with my free hand and give him a little smile, which seems to satisfy him; he turns his attention back to the display tables.

The dog-man's attention hasn't wavered from my *revensell*. His lips are pulled back, exposing some wicked canines. He's salivating and producing a low growl from the back of his throat.

As I inspect him further, I notice what poor shape he's in. I can see the outline of his bones through the skin on his legs and arms. His collarbones are pressing against the tanned flesh of his chest. This male is starving to death in front of my eyes!

My glance darts to the twins and I catch Braxx's eye. He's happy as always as he holds up a knife of some sort. I assume he's picked something he wants to buy. I can't help but remember how emaciated he was when he first came on board. He'd been so poorly treated, so abused he was close to death.

My eyes skitter to the male squatting in this open field. I don't know if he's even aware of my existence. He seems focused only on the meat clutched in my hand.

I take one tiny step forward and his eyes widen as his haunches lift higher, as if he'll pounce the moment I get within the circle of his metal chain.

He's staked to the ground, as well as wearing a pain/kill collar. He's drooling more profusely now, deep growling noises are escaping from his mouth.

"Shut the *drack* up!" an angry male voice yells from under the blanket tent.

"Um," I call. "Uh, sir, may I feed this…" I don't know what to call the being on the chain.

A shaggy head and rotund torso protrude from the makeshift tent. He's a heavy, porcine humanoid with upthrust tusks and rounded eyes. His belly and arms are huge and beefy, yet his legs are almost spindly. He's old, with wrinkles that lie in thick, dirty folds. By the look of him, that face hasn't smiled in a long time.

"Stand back, female. That geneslave's a guard animal. He'll maul you if you get too close."

"He looks hungry."

"He is. He's always hungry. He'd eat half my paycheck if I let him."

"I'm done with my *revensell*." I hold it up; I've taken maybe ten bites. "Mind if I give it to him?"

"Sure, I'll take it off your hands," his voice is as oily as the rest of him.

"I'd like to give it to him myself if that's okay. What's his name?"

"Don't have no name. I call him *Drack*. I'll take that meat." He points to the haunch with his filthy double chin.

How do I keep the food away from this asshole and get it to the poor...geneslave?

"He reminds me of my pet at home. I'd like to give it to him myself."

The male on the chain seems completely uninterested in the verbal exchange between me and his owner. His eyes haven't left the meat.

"Do what you want you crazy bitch," the male says, then lazily ducks back into his tent.

I glance over and see Axx and Braxx in sober deliberations as they haggle with their shopkeeper. I know they'll blow a gasket if they discover I'm doing this, so I move quickly.

I'm not stupid. I'm not getting close enough for those sharp canines to take a bite out of me. I grab a long stick off the ground nearby, wipe it on the inside hem of my dress, and poke it through the thickest part of the meat.

"Here you go, boy." I lift the stick toward him and edge closer.

For the first time, his gaze leaves the food. He looks me straight in the eyes. I don't know what a geneslave is, but I am absolutely certain he's a sentient being. There's intelligence in those large brown eyes.

My feet don't leave the path. I'm not getting closer until I see how close that chain will allow him to get to me.

"Come on, boy. Come toward me until your chain is tight."

Perhaps he understands me, because he approaches me on all fours. The chain isn't tight yet, though.

"Hurry." I glance at the guys. It looks like they're almost done with their purchase. Somehow I know they'll disapprove of me getting even this close to that drooling mouth full of sharp teeth.

He inches closer until the chain pulls at his throat, then comes a bit closer, as if to prove he's at the end of his tether.

"There you go. Good boy." I extend my stick just far enough for him to grab the meat with his hands. The whole time I'm coaching myself to just drop the stick if he tries to grab it and yank me toward him.

I shouldn't have worried, though. He slides the meat off, turns his back to the tent and proceeds to inhale the meat at a shocking rate. The smacking noises he's making are nauseating, but I guess they're a product of getting as much food down your throat in the least amount of time possible.

"Did that stupid bitch give you all that meat, boy?" I hear from the sullen slaver. He pokes his greasy, snarled head out of the tent and moves to the male with surprising speed.

It's like watching a race where you desperately want one contestant to win. I want the male on the ground to scrape every morsel off the bone before the approaching asshole gets to him. No wonder the geneslave was inhaling that meat. He knew he had less than a minute to get his fill before it was yanked away.

"Give me that, you piece of shit." The old man kicks him soundly in his side. It doesn't stop the dog-man, though. He just lies on the ground, his back toward his owner, and keeps tearing as much meat off the bone as is possible before the slaver touches the controller on his wrist to activate the geneslave's pain/kill collar.

The geneslave lets out an agonized yelp, yet somehow keeps getting food into his mouth until the second shock. All his muscles go stiff as an unearthly pain-filled howl escapes his lips. Then he goes limp.

I must have screamed because Axx and Braxx are running toward me. I realize I have tears snaking down my cheeks. Although my captors never activated my collar, I've worn one. I can only imagine how painful that must have been for the male lying motionless on the ground.

"Are you okay?" Braxx asks as he leans his face into mine, eyes wide in fright.

I glance over to see Axxios nearby, gun drawn, ready to protect me.

"I'm fine, guys. It's just…" I point to the supine figure on the ground. The old shithead must be back in his tent. "That male was starving. I gave him my *revensell*. His owner shocked him to steal the meat out of his hands."

Axx, gun in hand, walks closer to inspect the male on the ground. "He's a geneslave, Brianna. What were you thinking? How close did you get?"

"I gave him the meat on a stick when he was at the end of his chain. I'm not stupid. What's a geneslave?"

Braxx's arm circles my waist as he explains, "The Federation is rumored to be doing genetic experiments. I've heard they throw genetic material into a test tube, let it gestate, destroy the obvious deformities, and raise the rest. Sounds like they're trying to breed the perfect soldier.

"They deny they're doing such things, but rumor has it the Feds call them 'Products.' Folks around the galaxy call them 'geneslaves'. "

Axx stalks over, flanks my other side, pulls me toward him, and presses a close-lipped kiss to my temple. I look at him, one brow raised in question. I've seen Axx in many moods. Most of them naked and sweaty. I've never seen him tender before.

His response to my unspoken question is to give me a soft kiss on my mouth. "Don't worry us like that again, Angel. Let's all get back to the *Slacker* alive today," he chuckles.

"We can't leave him here. That old fucker is going to kill him. Look how thin he is."

"We can't bring every stray we find back on board our vessel, Brianna. Besides, geneslaves are part animal. We have no idea what that thing is capable of," Braxx says.

"Look at him, Braxx. You were an inch away from death, and you weren't even as thin as he is. He's being beaten regularly, he's malnourished. Don't you feel for him?"

"Feel for him? Yes. Want to bring an unknown alien aboard our ship? No." He shakes his head. "Besides, Captain Zar won't allow it. He wouldn't even let Petra come on board and she's an Earth female. She had to buy her way onto our vessel. Our resources are limited."

"Please?" Oops, did I really say that? Was I asking like a five-year-old asks her parents to bring home a stray?

"Did he speak to you, Brianna?" Axxios asks. "Is he even capable of speech? Is he a sentient being or just an animal?"

How odd that Braxx is the harsher of the two, and Axx is trying to persuade me with logic.

"No."

"Earth must have been a wonderful paradise if every injustice bothers you so much. The rest of the galaxy isn't such a nice place. There's war and famine and slavery here. We can't right every wrong or correct every abuse, Angel," Axx says. "I'm sorry you can't fix everything you see that pulls at your heart."

I look at him to see if he's mocking me, but his face is full of sweet concern. He kisses my forehead, like he's bestowing all his strength and affection on me. This gesture is so tender my knees weaken. I have to reach up and hold onto his strong arms to steady myself.

"We can't fix this, Angel. I'm sorry," he whispers in my ear and pulls me down the pathway.

I look back, the male is still lying in the dirt, unmoving. I keep telling myself there's nothing I can do, but my stomach churns with guilt.

Chapter Ten

Axxios

Looking back, I think I'd noticed some changes before I saw the evidence of Braxx's erection the other night. But the fact that my silver had an erection proves Brianna's our bondmate.

I had suspicions the moment I saw her. She's the exact image painted on the rotunda of our room. But that could have been a fluke. It wasn't surprising when Braxx called her 'Angel.' How could he not?

But things have been changing inside me since Braxx came out of his coma. I'm more tuned in to Brianna's moods as well as my own. When I stroke myself I imagine kissing her more and holding her after—which I never did before. Here on Fairea I've noticed my protective instincts are off the charts.

I'd always wondered what would happen when...if...we found our bondmate. For most Mythrians, nothing changes for the gold. He continues to make most of the decisions, he maintains his aggressive drives, and his sexual appetites don't change unless they increase.

It's the silver who does most of the transforming. He develops a sex drive while maintaining his ability to connect to his emotions.

Some golds, however, develop a closer connection to their emotional side. I think that's happening to me. And I'm not certain I like it. I don't want to lose my edge. I don't want to become weak. I'm the one who ultimately has to protect everyone.

But I have to admit, Brie's softening toward me today. She's definitely letting down her guard, and that feels fantastic.

Her delicate, little hand snags mine and nestles in my grip. I look over at her and catch her smiling at me. Her actions seem effortless and unaffected. She simply seems happy to be in my presence. I've never known her to act this way before. She's holding Braxx's hand in her right and mine in her left and looking around at all the chaotic hubbub as if it's the most fascinating place she's ever seen.

"Did you each buy a knife? I want to see," she demands.

Braxx eagerly pulls her off the path between two booths so we don't get trampled. As the day's gone by the crush of people has gotten worse.

"Look, Brie," Braxx says excitedly, "I've never seen one like this. I think they're only sold on the black market—and here." He pulls out his knife. It's about eight inches long, with a black metal blade. "But look!" He presses a button under the guard and the blade illuminates and turns red, converting it into a laser.

"Can I see?" Brianna reaches out to touch it, but Braxx immediately pulls it away. "Super dangerous, Brie. This could slice off your fingers."

Brianna pulls her hand back as if it was burned. "Whoa, I wasn't thinking."

He keeps a steady hold on the knife, but steps closer so he can show her where the hidden mechanism is.

"Cool," she says.

"Right, lasers don't get hot."

"Oh," she laughs, "on Earth 'cool' means neat."

Braxx looks confused.

"Okay, I'll turn into a human thesaurus. Cool means good, interesting, excellent."

"Got it! You and this knife are cool."

"Axxios, make him stop complimenting me. He's new at this. Teach him the rules."

"Great idea, Brianna. Since Braxx is new, let's make new rules. We can vote on them. All in favor of forbidding the use of the word beautiful say yes."

"Yes."

"I only hear one 'yes,' you're outvoted," I pronounce. "All in favor of restricting compliments to the beautiful lady say yes."

"Yes."

"I only hear one 'yes,' you're outvoted." I nod my head with finality.

"All in favor of no more massages, say yes." I spear her with a look I hope is so blatant, so unambiguous she couldn't possibly interpret it as anything other than the shameless proposition that it is.

"Yes."

"I only hear one 'yes,'" Braxx joins in the fun, but his eyes are burning with desire. What a revelation, to see my silver flirting shamelessly. I can't wait to see more of his transformation. "You're outvoted."

"Are you having fun with us Axx? I wish you could see your face. There." She points at a hat shop two stalls down and pulls me until I'm standing in front of a mirror. "Look at yourself."

I peer at myself in the mirror. I haven't seen this look on my face since I was a gray. I'm happy. The corners of my lips are turned up, my facial muscles are relaxed, and my eyes are sparkling.

Realizing I haven't experienced joy in twenty years makes my chest ache. Really? Has being a gold turned me to stone? I'd never acknowledged it before, but I always envied Braxx. Being silver, he never had the pressure I did. He could be childish and silly and have fun.

When Braxx was still in a coma, Dr. Drayke showed me scans of my twin's long bones. The doc said he's never seen anyone who'd been so badly tortured. I haven't had the heart to ask him about it, nor has Braxx mentioned it. I'd take the pain for him if I could. It's what golds do.

You'd never know what he'd been through by looking at him. He's his usual happy self. This proves he's stronger than I ever gave him credit.

Gods! I love my brother. I reach over and pull him to me so quick and hard he falls against me to keep from tipping over. "I love you, gem. I never forgave myself when I saw your ship blow up. I thought you were dead. I took responsibility. I'm so glad you're alive." I squeeze him tight.

Instead of embarrassing him and causing him to pull away, he hugs me back. Perhaps he gave his staff to Brie because he's got me in an impossibly tight hug. "I love you, too, Axx. I've missed you since you became a gold. You pulled away. Our bond was never the same. I felt abandoned."

He puts his lips to my ear, "This is the tri-bond, right? You have...emotions again? I get my brother back? I love you." He pats my back.

I'm pulled back to the present when the shopkeeper clears his throat loudly enough to be heard two stalls down. I step back, make certain Braxx has his staff in his hand, then step completely away.

The three of us leave the little shop and huddle in an open space between two stalls. I remember when we were young enough to play with blocks. I recall toppling a building and using the very same blocks to construct a completely different structure. That's what I feel like right this minima— like I've been cracked apart, disassembled and I'm in the process of being completely rearranged.

Brianna's hand finds mine. I open my eyes to see her clutching Braxx's hand in her other. Braxx throws his arm around my shoulder and I mirror his action, careful not to hurt his back. The three of us are in a circle—connected. Perhaps I'm hallucinating, but I feel energy circling between the three of us. The speed and intensity rises with each circuit.

"Whoa!" Briana says. "I feel like I drank a pint of whiskey." She pulls her hands away and puts her palms to her cheeks. "Maybe I'm getting sick."

I don't want to tell her I think this is the bond. I think it would alarm her. Besides, this isn't the time or place.

"Maybe it's the heat," I suggest while fanning her with my hand.

"Yeah, I think I'm already feeling better." She takes a deep breath and grins. "All in favor of Axxios being able to call Brie 'Brie' say yes," she says, smiling at me like she could kiss me right here in front of a thousand aliens on this dirt path.

"Yes!" the three of us shout at once. Then she kisses me. She just stepped right over, reached up on her toes, tugged my head down to hers and planted her lips solidly on mine.

I pull her farther back between the stalls. I want this kiss, I want it to be good, and I want it to be private. Braxx stands between us and the main pathway, but he doesn't turn his back on us to allow privacy, he watches. If Brie was more familiar with Mythrian ways, she'd include him. But that would be too much to expect.

I tune out everything but Brie. I pull away for a moment and allow myself the luxury of drinking in the way she looks. Her curves in that dress could wake the dead. Her hair, braided into a crown accentuates the green of her uptilted eyes. And those eyes, they are looking at me impatiently, with longing, in a way they never have before.

We've known each other for two months and rutted many times, but I've never seen this look on her face before. A look that says she can't wait to be in my arms.

I lift her up and crush her to my chest. Before I kiss her again, though, I whisper in her ear. "I apologize for any wrongs I've done you, Brie." Her name tastes like honey on my lips. "I gave you everything I was able. I will always give you everything I'm able."

Now I drag my lips slowly across her velvety skin from her ear to the corner of her mouth. Funny, sex always felt like a sprint before, like a race to the finish line. Now I want it to be a marathon. I want to enjoy the journey along the way.

I nibble the corner of her mouth, then work my way inward so slowly I feel her impatience. I slide my tongue along the seam of her lips and am elated when she opens herself to me. The tip of her tongue flicks mine, then we engage in mock battle. I learned these moves in captaincy school, but my studies were never this enjoyable.

Advance and then retreat. She makes a low moan in the back of her throat when I retreat, then she advances into the warmth of my mouth.

"You taste delicious, Brie," I moan against her lips. "I apologize if I never told you that before."

I kiss her closed lips, then enjoy breaching her threshold again. There are other thresholds I'm dying to breach, but this is a marathon. We have all the time in the galaxy for that. The three of us do.

I reach my hand into the long, thick, brown hair that was never pulled into her braid. I'm kissing her more forcefully now, plundering and taking my pleasure from her. From the low moans she's emitting from the back of her throat, I'm giving as well as receiving.

Her hands move from where they've been planted on my shoulders slowly down my back to rest on the exposed globes of my ass. She presses me against her, my engorged cock captured against her belly.

"Two security guards on hovercraft are approaching," Braxx interrupts. "We should probably get to the *mronck* exhibition if we're going to attend."

I pull away to catch a look at Brie before she shutters her expression. She looks mesmerized, lost, with a faraway expression in her eyes. I know this female. Is she going to doubt herself? Re-examine her own emotions? Question her decision to let me in?

"All in favor of going to the mronck show say 'yes,'" she says.

"Yes," we all reply, then move back into the path toward the arena.

"Um...all in favor of never mentioning what just happened say 'yes,'" she says.

Other than her voice, neither of us chime in.

"What's happening is wonderful," Braxx says with authority. "We don't need to name it, or quantify it or do scientific experiments on it. Let's just let go, explore, and see what happens."

Brianna

That kiss must have put us behind schedule because we're almost jogging to the exhibition. There are so many people on the pathway it's hard for the three of us to push our way through the press of flesh—and spikes and scales.

I'm holding both their hands, Axx in front, parting the sea of people, Braxx behind. This gives me a moment to contemplate what just happened back there.

I'm a bit hazy and confused; that happened before the kiss. I glance ahead at Axx, his golden skin glistening in the sun—and there's a lot of it exposed in the loincloth and skimpy black leather outfit he's wearing. It's no secret that I'm attracted to him, I thought he was gorgeous the first moment I saw him. Well, not the exact first moment I saw him. That moment was filled with terror. I'd just been kidnapped from my bed and thrown into a cell with a huge metal-looking alien.

It was shortly after my pumping adrenaline slowed that I realized how gorgeous he is. But that kiss just now? The one I initiated? That was amazing. I've never experienced that level of intimacy with him before. I shake my head as we run through a muddy area strewn with hay.

And Braxx? He just stood back and watched us kiss for goodness sake. Does this mean I'm falling into a relationship with the two of them?

There's no time for me to explore this further, the circle of flags billowing in the wind up ahead must signal we're almost there. Axx pays our entry fee, then wends his way toward the front. The stadium reminds me of the setup for a rodeo back home. There's an oval area a little larger than a football field that's filled with leveled, red dirt. Rows of benches surround it, stepped up higher and higher so all the seats have a good view.

But Axx seems intent on procuring the best seats. We arrive at the front row, which isn't full. There's a little amphibious creature standing in front of the seats, facing the crowd. I can't tell whether it's male or female. It's in a gray jumpsuit with a horse's head logo on it.

"How much?" Axx asks.

"For three? One-hundred twenty credits." It sticks out a warty, khaki-colored hand, and the transaction is completed in a second.

"Did you just bribe him for these seats?" Why this, out of everything I've seen today, surprises me I have no idea.

"Yes, nothing but the best for *Brie*," he emphasizes my name, like he loves the feel of it on his tongue.

"All in favor of paying extra credits for the good seats say yes," Braxx says.

"Yes," is shouted by two male voices.

"Brie's outvoted. Let's enjoy it," Braxx pronounces.

I'm too antsy to sit, so I go to the stockade fence a few feet in front of us and look out at the arena. Not much to see but red dirt at the moment. When I turn around I see my two guys flanking my spot on the bench. They're both looking expectantly at me, like I'm the most interesting thing in the entire arena.

My stomach does an interesting somersault in slow motion, my hands and jaw clench. Is this really happening? Am I entering into a relationship with two guys? Two gorgeous guys who have been nothing but sweet to me? I gaze into two sets of turquoise eyes. They're not looking at me like a man on the street looks at a woman he wants to proposition. No, they're looking at me the way a man looks at a woman he likes, and admires, and enjoys and...wants to propose to.

Fear arrows through me and goes straight to clench in my belly. I never saw this coming.

I hear the blare of trumpets and take my seat. A silver hand grabs my right, and a gold snags my left, and then I focus on what's happening in the arena.

Four green-skinned males dressed in colorful silk slacks and shirts play a rousing rendition of peppy music on large brass instruments as the huge crowd hushes itself quiet.

"Males and females," a hidden female announces, "welcome to our exhibition."

And with that, a procession of amazing animals and people enter the arena. The *mroncks* look like horses in every way except they have six legs. It takes a full minute of watching their feet move before I can focus on anything else. You'd think they'd look clumsy or stumble, but their movements are graceful.

For a moment I'm reminded of that scene in *The Wizard of Oz* when they finally arrive at Emerald City and they see "a horse of a different color," because that's what I'm seeing. There's a stunning green one with a mustard-yellow mane and tail, a blood-red with midnight black mane and tail, and a cobalt blue with turquoise hair.

"Wow, guys, they're so gorgeous," I say without taking my eyes off the spectacle. And it *is* a spectacle. The trumpets are still blaring, and the people are leading the horses by their bridles. The males and females in the arena are every shape and size, all wearing silky uniforms of every color and description. The whole extravaganza is total eye candy.

The first act consists of six of the animals, each with a male and female pair standing on top of its back. It starts out slow and graceful, but by the end, they're racing and zigzagging so fast I realize I'm clutching the guys' hands in excitement.

For the next act, they let about twenty *mronk*s loose in the huge arena. At first, they just mill around, nosing the dirt for a blade of grass. Then a willowy female, maybe six feet tall and one hundred pounds is carried in on a fancy litter. Dressed in a gauzy dress, she jumps down and stalks around the arena like she owns it. The animals immediately lift their heads, focus on her, and walk toward her.

Then the animals, begin to move in unison with no discernible cue from the trainer. At first, they simply move from one end of the area to the other, as if pulled by invisible strings. Then they do increasingly complex tasks like walking in a circle, then in unison, changing direction.

By the end of the act, they're galloping in perfect formation. The final task is what we used to call "thread the needle," where horses come from opposite directions. When they merge, they alternate who goes first with perfect precision. Of course, I've only seen this before where there were human riders giving the cues. My mind is boggled that the animals are doing this without riders and seemingly without physical or verbal direction of any kind.

I tear my eyes from the spectacle for half a second to check on the guys, and see both of them are watching me with amused expressions on their faces. They're getting more of a kick out of my enjoyment of the performance than the performance itself.

"Like it, Brie?" Braxx asks, his voice deep and low near my ear.

"I love it." I have a huge smile plastered on my face.

I enjoy the rest of the show, but that was definitely my favorite act. I still can't figure out how she did it. Maybe she had telepathy with the *mroncks*. When I get home I'll have to ask Tyree, who's psychic, if he can communicate with animals.

When the show is over, we wait until the stands empty out. We're in the front row, no need to fight through the crowd to leave.

"That was fantastic!" I gush. "Did you guys see this when you were kids?"

"I couldn't get over the female communicating with the *mroncks* all those years ago," Axx says, "and I still don't understand how she does it."

"It's the same female?"

"Looks identical, but maybe it's her daughter."

"There are so many things in this universe I don't understand," I admit.

"Thirsty, Angel?" Braxxus asks.

I nod.

"I think you'd like *premmod*. It's tart and sweet and quenches your thirst."

"Sounds like lemonade. That would be perfect."

The three suns are all high in the sky and look close to converging, even though they all started far from each other this morning when we got off the ship. I hadn't noticed because I'd been so fascinated by the performance, but I'm melting in this dress.

"Let's get a drink and find some shade," I say as the crowd thins out.

As we're walking up the steps to leave the arena I notice two of the deepest cuts on B's back are weeping.

"Braxx, you're bleeding," my voice is alarmed.

We stop and both Axxios and I inspect. We don't want to pull off the plas-film to look closer, we have nothing to replace it with.

"It doesn't look serious to me, what do you think Brie?" Axxios asks.

"It was a lot worse a few days ago, but I don't think it should be bleeding at this point in his recovery. Should we call Dr. Drayke?"

"I think we should just make our way back to the ship," Axx pronounces. "We'll take our time, take it easy."

"Do I get a say in this?" Braxx asks.

"No," Axx and I reply in unison.

"I'm not ruining Angel's day because of a trickle of blood," Braxx insists.

"All in favor of returning to the ship say yes," I say.

"Yes," Axx and I respond.

"Braxx is outvoted. Let's get a drink and work our way to the *Slacker*."

The two guys are looking at each other seriously, not taking their eyes off each other. I'm going to have to get some clarification when we're back on the ship. Are they having a silent psychic conversation? Is this the Mythrian twin thing Axx kept talking about?

We're sitting on a bench, drinking our *premmods*, which are indistinguishable from lemonade, and eating an intergalactic version of something resembling fried okra. I have no intention of investigating the nature of its ingredients.

The guys forgot to distract me and have me seated directly across from a stall with a huge picture of a *reven*. I never thought Axx knew me very well, but he was right on the mark when he tried to keep me from getting an eyeful of the poor thing.

It reminds me of that scene in *The Fly* where some animal goes into a machine and comes out dead with half its insides on its outsides. The *reven* looks inside out and hairy and bloody and gross. I shiver. It's repugnant.

Until I saw it I had my eye on a cheesecakey-looking thing at one of the other booths, but I've lost my appetite. I'm still shuddering when we hear a commotion from our left.

It takes my brain a few seconds longer than the guys to grasp what's going on. It sounds like explosions!

Axx and Braxx have pulled their guns and are already standing before my brain is fully engaged. "Braxx, take point!" Axxios yells over the din of the explosions and cacophony of people yelling. Axx pushes me in front of him and the three of us take off at a run toward the ship.

I hear screaming behind us. It's clear from the noise that people are being hurt, possibly killed. I don't spare a minute looking backward. I just keep my eyes focused ahead and follow B.

"Jog left," Axx orders from behind. I assume he wants us away from the herd so we don't get trampled. He's directing us back to the more sparsely-traveled paths we came in on.

Lasers have a high-pitched whine when they're fired. That's not what I'm hearing. It's more like the bombs or mortar rounds I've heard in movies about Vietnam. Fear spikes up my spine. I'm worried not only for myself but for my guys. Braxx's plas-film is now filled with blood, and some is trickling out the bottom. There's no time to mention it and nothing we can do about it. We just have to keep running.

I smell smoke and something terrible I assume is alien gunpowder. I hear the surreal sound of people shouting behind me. The muscles in my calves are burning from running without a break. I'm trembling with terror, but still moving forward.

I realize Axx put Braxx in front for a reason. He's the weakest link, and that person should always be at the front of the line so he doesn't fall behind. His pace is slowing and he's leaning on his staff harder with every step.

I have no idea how far it is to the ship, I'm just following Braxx's bloody back and trying not to totally freak out. Braxx stops in his tracks and turns around. When I follow his gaze I see Axx is down on the ground—he's been hit! Braxx must have felt Axx's pain through his twin bond.

"*Drack*!" Braxx shouts as we run back to Axx. He's sprawled on his stomach in the dirt path. He's still alive, but unconscious. It's clear he's been badly hurt. His back is peppered with bleeding cuts. Some look deep. My heart clenches in pain. I care for him. I don't want him to die.

Braxx tosses his staff into the dirt, kneels down on one knee and scoops up his brother. I can't imagine this will work. Axx probably outweighs him by forty pounds and Braxx is weak and bleeding already. I don't say a word, I'm not stupid enough to believe for a moment that Braxxus won't do everything in his power to help his gem.

There's nothing I can do to help, so I just keep quiet and jog next to Braxxus. Blood is pouring from his back now, the plas-film isn't holding back the flow. Braxx isn't running so much as lurching down the road, favoring one leg.

The sound of gunfire or explosions sounds closer. I'm not sure any of us are going to make it. My pulse is hammering and my throat is on fire, but I keep moving forward.

We're not jogging anymore, just walking, our pace slowing with every step. Braxx probably isn't even aware that he grunts every time his right foot hits the ground. The sound and even the sensation of the bomb concussions are getting closer. I can't imagine we'll get out of these fairgrounds alive.

"Angel, go right at the end of this aisle. You'll see the flags at the entrance. Head there and then out to the airfield. Don't stop until you're on board. Remember where we are so you can tell Zar. Go!"

"No." He's crazy if he thinks I'm leaving him.

"Angel," is all he says. I'm sure he doesn't have the energy to argue.

I look over to my left and see the dog-man. There's a panicked look on his face. He's standing up at the end of his tether, the chain straining.

"Let me go, I'll help you," he pleads, his round, brown canine eyes boring into mine.

I don't believe for a second he'll help, but it's obvious his owner abandoned him. He'll certainly die when whoever is detonating those bombs finds him staked to the ground.

I pull Braxx's new laser knife out of the sheath at his waist and run back toward the geneslave.

"No, Angel, he'll kill you!" Braxx yells. He's stopped moving and is coming back for me.

"Keep moving, Braxx. This will just take a second."

I don't wait to see what he does. The faster I get this done, the better. Frankly, I don't think any of us are going to make it. This male has the best chance of survival if I just cut his chain and let him run away.

"Hurry," he urges around his mouthful of sharp teeth.

My fingers instinctively find the hidden button that turns the knife into a laser and the red beam cuts the thick metal chain like butter.

Just as I'd assumed, he's racing before I can turn the laser off. I'm shocked when, instead of running away, he dashes straight to Braxx. In the matter of a moment, Axx's heavy frame is in the geneslave's arms.

The dog-man is a tall male with a big frame, but he's so emaciated Axx has to outweigh him by at least seventy pounds. The feds must know what they're doing, because malnourished or not, the geneslave is carrying Axx like he weighs no more than a puppy.

I catch up to Braxx, who's moving faster now that he's not carrying his gem. I grab his hand and place it on my shoulder. He tries not to put much of his weight on me as he hobbles to catch up to his brother.

"Right," Braxx shouts as we near the end of the aisle.

I see the flags signaling the entrance where we arrived. There's a crush of people trying to file through the narrow opening to evacuate the park. Now that we're close to others, I hear the word "terrorists" float over the other panicked noises of the crowd.

If they'd been smart, they would have stationed some of their comrades at this entrance and picked us off like shooting fish in a barrel as we come running out. Luckily, the only weapon fire I hear is behind us.

The *Slacker* is probably still a quarter-mile away at the airfield. The geneslave glances at Braxx, who points in the general direction and we're all off as fast as possible.

Braxx's back is bleeding profusely, blood trailing from under the plas-film down his thighs and into the dust. The geneslave's carrying Axx in his arms. I've seen enough war movies to know Axx has been hit by shrapnel, blood is dripping from his back, making thin red trails in the dirt.

I remember I have a wrist comm, and call the ship.

"We'll need a hover-stretcher," I say without preamble. "Axx and Braxx both need medical attention."

"Everyone but you is back on board," Callista informs me. "There are a few minor casualties, only one major. Stryker can grab a stretcher and meet you in the lot."

"Expect four of us."

"No strays, Brianna," it's Zar's stern voice. He must have overheard our conversation.

"He saved our lives. We'd all be dead in the dirt back there if he hadn't helped us."

"Can't put ourselves at risk. No."

A concussion shakes the ground beneath us—definitely closer than anything we've experienced before. Did I hear the geneslave grunt? I pick up the pace even though my muscles are screaming in pain.

I see Stryker hustling toward us guiding the hover-stretcher, his tall, scarred body shining in the suns. The geneslave gently lays Axx on it and Stryker hustles the stretcher up the ramp and into the waiting maw of the ship.

Braxx and I are panting, twenty feet from the ramp. Panicked sounds of the crowd reach us. The fight must have followed us into the parking area. We should be inside our ship and leaving atmo right this minute, but I can't leave the male who without a doubt saved our lives.

"I heard your comm," his gravelly voice rumbles in my ear. I hadn't realized he was so close. Braxx pulls me away from the dog-man, toward the awaiting ramp.

"It's okay. Don't risk your safety for me. Go." He walks away.

"No!" I say, even as Braxx gently tugs me toward the ship. "No, I'm not leaving him. He saved our lives. This isn't right!"

"Angel, we have to go." His weight is resting heavier on my shoulder, the sounds of the explosions are getting closer. I can see a parked hovercraft explode less than a city block away. There is no time for this.

"Zar, please," Braxx yells into his comm, "let us in. Let us all in before we die. We can drop him on the next planet. Let's argue about it later."

A moment's pause, then, "Okay, but there's a contingent of armed gladiators at the door."

"Hey!" I scream, but he's off running. "Geneslave!" I scream, wincing at the sound of the derogatory term coming out of my mouth.

He turns to look at me, still running in the other direction. "Come aboard," I motion to him. It's hard to tell, but I think that's a smile on his face.

Chapter Eleven

Brianna

We run up the ramp straight into the barrels of three lasers. Dax, the huge Neanderthal, would be imposing enough on his own, but strong, silver Steele is on one side, and heavily-muscled, heavily-scarred Shadow is on the other.

Only a crazy man would argue with these three, and the geneslave doesn't appear crazy. In fact, he sinks to his knees and puts his hands behind his head in complete surrender. I'm almost knocked to the floor as we take off, and again when we launch into hyperspace a moment later.

Stryker returns to the loading bay at a run, pushing the empty hover-stretcher. Braxxus balks for a moment, not wanting to get on it, but when I urge him, he lies down and we're off running through the halls.

When we arrive in medbay, I'm torn between checking on Axx, and holding Braxx's hand. There are only two exam rooms. Tall, white, Norse-god looking Theos is in one, with a very worried Savannah at his bedside. I'd like to console her, but she's crying and I'm distracted with my guys. I'll catch her later.

Axx is in the other exam room, lying on his side facing the far wall. Some of the blood has been sponged off his back, but the medbot hasn't begun to clean or stitch any of his injuries. And by the look of things, there are a lot of them. Two of the wounds are gaping open and blood is pouring out onto the absorbent pad on the mattress. My throat constricts in worry just seeing the extent of the damage.

Dr. Drayke is consulting his medpad, Nova at his side. Or...is there a word that indicates closer than at someone's side? She's practically glued to his hip. I wonder if this is the only way he can function without the trembling hands and brain fog he'd complained of the other day.

The doc hurries over to Braxx, gives a perfunctory look at his back, and asks, "Any new injuries?"

"No," Braxx croaks.

"You, Brianna? Any injuries?"

I shake my head no.

"Axx is the most serious injury at the moment. I'll address his wounds, then get to you, Braxx. I'll keep you out in the hallway for now."

Braxx grabs my hand and squeezes it. "Don't worry, Angel, everything will work out, it always does." He smiles weakly at me.

"You said that before, how can you be so sure?"

"'Cause we found our angel. The Galaxy has conspired to bring us together. It wouldn't go to all that trouble just to pull us apart, would it?"

I bite back a cynical retort. He doesn't need to hear my cynicism right this moment.

"Things are better between you and Axx now, right?" Despite all the pain he's in, this seems to be his primary concern.

I pause a moment to consider his question. A montage of pictures of Axx's handsome face flashes through my mind, but the question isn't about whether I find him attractive, of course I do, who wouldn't?

But he's changed, something's happened to him since his brother came out of his coma. He's more...alive, more able to experience his emotions.

I dig even deeper into myself. Even if he wasn't in touch with his emotions, I have to admit I'd like him. The problem was I liked him *too* much. I didn't want to love without being loved in return. But after the blazing kiss we shared in the alleyway and his protection and concern at every turn, that doesn't seem like it's going to be a problem.

And then I realize what I just said. I used the "L" word. Holy shit, do I love him? We've been through a whirlwind together, that's true. But love?

"Angel?" Braxx interrupts the hamster-wheel of my thoughts. "You had to think way too long. You don't like Axx, that's okay." He pats my hand.

But by the look on his face—like his dog died and his pickup truck broke and his boss fired him and his house burned down—I don't think it's okay at all.

"Hey," I lean close and give a sweet kiss to those pale pink lips. "My thoughts are spinning, B. We were almost killed less than an hour ago. I'm worried sick about both of you. My relationship with your brother is far more complicated than how I feel about you. But yes, I think my problems with Axx are behind me." I kiss him again. "Are you in pain? After caring for you the last few weeks I know how to give a pain shot."

"Actually yes, but I'll wait to hear what Dr. Drayke says about Axx's condition before I dull my senses."

Less than ten minutes later, the medbot arm has cleaned Axx's back with an antiseptic solution and is now hard at work plucking out shrapnel.

My shit detector turns up to full blast when I see the doc hand Nova a hazmat suit, then climb into one himself. My hand is trembling in Braxx's grip, my eyes wide in terror.

The doc comes out into the hall, Nova at his side, and closes the door behind him. "We have some intel—what we heard over security comms from the ground, and now we're hearing from other ships that escaped Fairea the same time as us.

"It appears it was some type of terrorist activity. Who knows why they targeted a harmless planet that provides recreation? If we wanted to, I'm certain we could find some manifesto littered with poor grammar in the bowels of the Intergalactic Database.

"The bottom line is...not only were they lobbing antiquated pipe bombs at the fair-goers, the bombs were filled with shrapnel. If that wasn't bad enough, some of the shrapnel was irradiated."

I touch my hand behind my right ear as if I could make certain my translator was working properly. "Radiation, doc? Does that mean what it does on Earth?" It dawns on me that I needn't have asked, he's wearing a hazmat suit.

"Radiation can be deadly if the exposure is prolonged. Is that what it means to you?"

I nod slowly, a sinking feeling in my stomach. "So Axxios has irradiated shrapnel in his back? Theos, too?"

He shakes his head. "We checked him. Theos hasn't been contaminated, he'll be fine. Here's my plan. First, the medbots will remove all of Axxios's shrapnel, then jettison it immediately and get it off the vessel.

"There are medication regimens we can follow to minimize the damage caused by the radiation. I'm hoping this will all be a bad dream in a week or two. In the meantime, I don't want anyone in Axxios's exam room without one of these hazard protection suits on." He raises his voice and uses a tone I've never heard come out of his mouth before. "This means you, Nova." Never underestimate the protectiveness of a bonded male.

"I'm going to administer pills to you to minimize any possible effects you may have received from being in close proximity to the fragments. I—"

He's interrupted by a vile sound coming from Axx's room. The doc is up and in the exam room before I can blink. Braxx is struggling to get off his gurney, but I stop him. "You can't go in there, B. You'd have to be in a hazmat suit. Let's wait a moment and see what's going on."

Five minutes later, the doc comes out with a bright yellow medical waste bag. "One of the symptoms of radiation poisoning is nausea and vomiting," he says as he double bags it and puts it in the medical waste chute.

The doc comms the bridge and within minutes every person on the ship has been scanned for radioactivity. No one has been exposed except for Axxios. I sigh in relief.

"Brianna," Doctor Drayke says, "I'm going to ask you to leave, it's just too chaotic in here. I—"

"Doc," Zar's voice interrupts over the comm, "You've got an incoming. No one checked on the prisoner. Evidently, he got hit pretty bad when he was carrying Axxios. Steele tells me he lit up the radiation detection device almost to the max. He'll be handcuffed to his gurney."

"*Drack*," Drayke mutters, his eyes looking at the ceiling as if the answers to all his questions were written there. "Listen, everyone," he calls loudly enough for all to hear. "This medbay just wasn't built for an event like this. I need everyone's cooperation.

"Stryker," he barks into his wrist comm, "Come to medbay and help Savannah get Theos to his cabin." To Savannah he says, "I'm asking you to watch him for the next few days. I'll stop by your room to check on him before I go to sleep tonight no matter how late it is.

"Brianna, Braxxus is already on a stretcher. Grab some plas-film from the supply cabinet as well as antiseptic and cleaning supplies and take care of him in his room, it's larger than yours. I'll stop by later tonight. You've done this before, you should be fine."

I nod. I'm totally capable of this and glad to have something to do.

"Nova, I want you in our room. It's too dangerous here with radiation and a prisoner." Almost as an afterthought, he asks, "Who's the *dracking* prisoner?"

"My project," I admit, so guilty my voice is whisper soft. I hadn't realized my choice would put my friends in danger.

"Who?"

"A geneslave who helped us get to the *Slacker*."

"My dear Lord God Anteros," the blue doctor says. "You're leaving me in medbay with a geneslave? What type?"

"Appears canine," Braxx grits in pain.

"Zar," Drayke speaks into his comm. "I'll need round-the-clock security even if the geneslave is cuffed to the bed."

"I'm already arranging it," is Zar's clipped reply.

Braxxus

I'm lying on my stomach on my bed within ten minutes. Angel's gentle hands have washed me and are now dabbing at my tender flesh with a soft towel. I'm barely aware of any of it, though. I'm trying to get through to Axx through our twinlink. Nothing.

"You probably need stitches on two of these. Everything tore loose on that wild run back to the ship. Don't worry, I'll fashion some butterfly bandages out of the supplies I snagged before we left medbay. They'll hold you together. They don't have a medbot to spare."

I don't want to mention that the stitches tearing open on my back are nothing compared to what the Glee'non did during my captivity. Her voice sounded forlorn. I imagine she's feeling guilty that the geneslave is taking up a bed that could belong to me.

"Don't feel bad, Brie. That thing risked its life to carry Axx to the ship. It didn't have to. It could have run in the other direction. It made sure to bring up the rear in an effort to protect us both. I've got to give it credit."

"Do me a favor, please don't call him it. I don't fully understand what a geneslave is, but he was clearly male, and clearly a sentient being. He spoke to me."

"Okay." I have nothing else to say right now. My head is spinning with worried thoughts about my gem.

She dabs my back with antiseptic, applies a layer of plas-film, and lets out a deep sigh.
"I think I should move in here until you're better. I don't want you to be alone."

She sucks in a breath, probably realizing how horrible that sounded, reminding me Axx isn't here.

"I'd like that, Brie." I don't say what's on the tip of my tongue, that we belong together, that she should sleep here every night.

"I'm going to take a shower and gather a few things from my room. Want your pain shot now? You can nap while I'm gone."

Yes. No. I don't know. I'm a terrible gem, sleeping while Axx is fighting for his life. "Yes."

~.~

I wake up with my arm around Brie's waist, pulling her tightly against me. I love her long, brown hair, which is fanned around her head, some of it ribboned across my shoulder. I breathe in deeply, it smells clean and fresh, like a field of flowers on a humid day back on Mythros.

That thought brings back memories of playing with Axx in the sprawling gardens behind the Governors' Mansion when we were kids. We knew every hidden nook and secret hiding place on the grounds. We waged imaginary war and fought battles with the enemy, and laid on the grass and watched the clouds. We were inseparable. Even our fathers remarked on how close our twinbond was.

We don't exactly speak inside each others' heads like I've read about psychic phenomenon in other species. We communicate in pictures. Well, pictures and emotions. We can send each other a visual along with an emotion and know what the other sees or knows or feels.

We knew when each other was bored. Of course, you didn't need a twinbond to know that; we were the Governors' boys at state functions, what child wouldn't be bored?

But we could feel each others' pain and longing and happiness and fear. And we loved each other so much that sometimes his pain became my own. I honestly don't recall any jealousy of Axx—even when he did better at sports, even when he turned gold. I always wanted the best for him.

It was hard for me when he became gold, his depth of emotion faded away and our connection seemed faulty. Now we've only had each other back a scant few days. It was wonderful experiencing the twinbond full blast. And now it's completely severed.

But I don't want to think about that right now. There's nothing I can do to make things better. I'm lying here with my Angel in my arms. I want to focus on that.

I breathe in deeply through my nose to bring myself back to the present. She smells sweet and warm. The skin at the back of her neck is partially exposed. I kiss it, then my tongue peaks out to lick it there. I don't know how to describe her taste. It simply tastes like Brianna.

Her head is lying on my bicep, I'm cradling her. I wrestle down the urge to cup her breasts, that wouldn't be right. I'd love to kiss her pink lips. I want to explore her lush curves, first with my hands, then my mouth. I want to discover the taste between her legs.

And then I realize the rock-hard erection I experienced for the first time the other night, the one that should be pressing into her soft rear right this moment, is absent. My cock is soft. I can't get hard without the twinlink.

I've never disappointed a Mythrian female by my lack of arousal. No female from my planet would expect anything like that from an unbonded silver. But Brianna doesn't understand our foreign biology. From what I've learned about her species, my lack of properly functioning equipment would be a serious disappointment to her. Every male's fondest wish is to satisfy his female. If I wasn't flaccid already, I would be after that sobering thought.

She stirs next to me then rolls onto her side, facing me—and smiles. It's a slow, languorous smile that starts almost shyly, then widens to a sexy grin.

"So handsome, Braxx. You're so warm," her words are slightly slurred and fuzzy, her eyes are heavy-lidded.

"I like you, Braxx." Her eyes shift from mine to my mouth, then she breaches the gap between us so slowly I could easily stop her if I wanted. But I don't.

Her lips are soft and pillowy against mine. The sounds we make together are wet and welcoming. We lean into each other, tasting, mingling.

Now that I've had the experience of masculine arousal, its absence is a palpable loss. This isn't the same, not as wild or all-consuming as I felt the day the three of us shared a massage.

My hand is pressing the back of her neck to pull her closer. Neither of us can get enough of these kisses, at first close-lipped, now open.

Our tongues are dancing with each other. We're like two people on the dancefloor who have just met, but whose bodies move together in perfect harmony.

My hands glide up and down, from the small of her back to her shoulders. I notice every curve and indent. I'm cataloging every detail, to play back later when I'm alone. After she realizes my deficiencies and rejects me.

I push those thoughts to the back of my mind and focus on the warm, willing female who's alive in my arms right now.

She presses her pelvis toward mine, but I jack back, wanting to prolong the mystery, wanting just a few more *minimas* of this, the bliss of this intimacy, even if it's an illusion.

"You're right," she says, pulling away. "I know it's not the way Mythrians behave." She scoots farther from me on the big bed. "That wasn't fair of me. I don't understand everything about the twin thing, but I know the magic number is three. I'm a shit. Here I am trying to seduce you when your gem is in medbay." She reaches out and gently cups my cheek in her palm, then pulls away. "Sorry."

"Nothing to be sorry for, Brie. Every cell in my body aches for you, too." Well, almost every cell. She's not the villain here. I am, for not admitting my inadequacies.

I see the way she looks at me. Hell, I don't need a written roadmap; what just happened in this bed made it indelibly clear what she wants. I can't give her that. In her culture, without my twin, I would be considered half a male.

Brianna

Luckily, Dr. Drayke interrupted that awkward conversation before I felt compelled to apologize again. As soon as we let him in he got right to the point.

"Sorry I waited so long to stop by, but I've been crawling through all the information on the Intergalactic Database. Not good." He shakes his head.

Great bedside manner, doc.

"I've removed all the irradiated shrapnel from the geneslave, and patched him up as well as I could. He was badly wounded, but will recover."

Long pause. The doctor's pinched blue face is tighter than usual. He rubs the back of his neck with his palm, then tells us the bad news. "Axxios's injuries were actually less severe than the mutant's, but there's a serious complication. There's a small fragment of shrapnel lodged next to his spinal column.

"We're in a difficult spot. If we leave the shrapnel in, he'll suffer from radiation sickness and possibly die. If we try to remove it, we could paralyze him. The metal is lodged between thoracic 6 and 7." He points to his middle back. "If things go wrong he'd be paralyzed from there down."

Braxx had been standing next to me listening to the news. He sits heavily on the bed, then rests his face in his hands. I settle in next to him and gently rub his thigh.

"Tyree's on the bridge, trying to find the nearest planet with Class One hospitals. The best we've found is a twenty-six *hoara* journey from here. That isn't optimal, but it's the best we can do other than perform surgery here on board the *Lazy Slacker*. If…" he pauses and waits for Braxx to give him eye contact, "you decide that we should do the surgery. Some would choose to leave the metal where it is." He shrugs, "It's up to you."

It seems as if Braxx transforms before my eyes. He stands to his full height and steals his muscles. The set of his jaw seems firmer; the look in his eyes is sharper.

"Leave the shrapnel in and it's certain death, right?"

"With the levels of radiation we've measured, I would say yes, he'll die from that."

"And the surgery? What are the odds of paralysis?"

"Fifty percent, maybe higher. The odds are the same if we rush him to Champion III or we do the surgery on board. The better performance we could expect from a top-notch hospital would be offset by the length of time it would take to get there."

Braxx's gaze is fixed on the floor. If I didn't know better, I'd think he was doing complex algebraic calculations in his head, he's totally focused.

"He'd hate being paralyzed. Hate it." He rubs his chin. "But you can't let him die. Can you start the procedure right away?"

"I thought that would be your choice," the doc says as he stands. "I've already instructed the medbot to calculate the entire procedure. By the time we get back to medbay, it should be ready to make the first incision. You *are* going to wait in medbay, right?"

Braxx nods.

"You can't be in the procedure room until the shrapnel is removed and safely disposed of, but you can wait in the hall."

"Brie," Braxx looks at me, "get some sleep, it's the middle of the night. I'll comm you when the procedure is complete."

"Like hell I'll wait here."

Chapter Twelve

Brianna

Braxx and I have been sitting for hours on two small, hard metal chairs in the little medbay anteroom. Dr. Drayke set up all the instructions for the medbot, moved Axxios into the operating room, and watched the first few minutes of the procedure.

"I'm tired, shaky, and sleep-deprived," the doc announces as he puts fresh sheets on the empty exam room bed. "I'm going to eat some nutrition bars and grab some sleep right here. The bot decontaminated the entire room. I believe the worst of the bonding sickness is over. I think I'll be okay without Nova.

"Don't hesitate to contact me if you need to, but the computer will wake me right before the procedure is complete. Feel free to go back to your rooms. I can have the computer contact you as well if you'd like."

"No," Braxx says forcefully. "I'll stay here." He looks at me, silently urging me to go lie down and get some rest. The tiny shake of my head is all the answer he needs. I don't want to leave Braxx's side. I know I provide him a bit of comfort. And I want to be here for Axx as well, although there's absolutely nothing I can do to help.

I glance into the second exam room and see that Stryker has commandeered the bed and relegated the geneslave to the floor, one hand and one leg cuffed to recessed bolts in the wall.

"We haven't eaten in hours, B. I'm going to forage in the kitchen. I'll be back in a few minutes." I kiss the top of his head and make it to the kitchen in record time. It's after two a.m. and the halls are serene and quiet. Even though everyone's my friend here, sometimes it's nice to have the run of the ship to myself.

I rummage in the two huge cold boxes in the meal prep area and don't find anything that looks better than school cafeteria mystery meat. I set up a quick assembly line to make kindapeanutbutter sandwiches. Fifteen sandwiches later, arms laden with sammies and fruit, I head back to medbay.

Stryker is snoring like a freight train, I'm certain he doesn't want food right this moment. Braxx and the doc are sleeping soundly and I hate to wake them. The geneslave's lying quietly on his back, eyes wide open and looking straight at me.

"Hungry?" I whisper.

He nods.

I toss him a napkin-covered sandwich. He unwraps it with his free hand and teeth, then inhales it. I'd forgotten how emaciated he is, and how he had to avoid kicks from his master to eat the *revensell* I'd thrown him.

I know he can talk, but he doesn't say a word. It's obvious he'd like another sandwich, and equally obvious he won't ask.

I toss him another. It, too, is gone in a few huge bites. His eyes haven't left mine.

I throw him a third. He scarfs it down.

"More?" I ask.

He nods. Once. The tiniest movement of his head.

"What's your name?"

He's quiet for a long time. His eyes don't leave mine.

"Honestly, I thought that was a pretty easy question," I laugh nervously.

Even though I just threw the conversation ball into his court, he obviously feels no need to answer my question. Maybe there are reasons why everyone hates these guys. Even Braxx, the nicest male on the ship, called him an "it." Although he can understand human speech, it doesn't necessarily mean he has any humanity.

Originally, I was going to give him a sandwich when he answered my question, a little behavior modification. But he's obviously not answering, and he's probably still hungry. Not to toss him another sammie would just be cruel. I throw him number four; he actually chews this time.

"Another?" I offer.

He nods. This time he leaves it on his chest, still wrapped in a napkin. He gives me a challenging look, almost daring me to try to take it back.

"I have ten more. There's enough for everyone. I'm not going to snatch your food. Here," I toss him two of the spiky fuchsia fruits that have become my favorite food (well, favorite after KFC which I don't think I'm going to get for a while).

He looks at them like he's an orphan and he just got an iPhone *and* a puppy for Christmas. Is his hand trembling? Are his eyes a little shinier or is it a trick of the light?

"We'll feed you. No one is going to steal your food. And we'll keep tending your injuries. I haven't thanked you, but you saved my friend's life. I don't know what we'll do with you. I'm new around here. But there must be a place for...people like you to be safe. I'll help find that place for you. And when you're ready, you can tell me your name."

I move to leave, but he's still staring at me so intensely I wait, sensing there's something he wants to say.

"Don't have one."

It takes me a moment to replay our conversation to my last question—his name.

"You don't have a name?" It's been a long day. I've been shot at and both the males I care about have been wounded, one perhaps mortally so. So I have no idea why this matter-of-fact statement from this poor male brings tears to my eyes.

"Well, give it some thought. I'd say it's high time you gave yourself one."

I walk into the little waiting area and see Braxxus in one of the two small, metal chairs that are sitting side by side. He's sound asleep, his head braced against the wall behind him. He has to be uncomfortable, but I doubt he could find a better position.

I put the plate on the floor in front of him so when he wakes up he'll see it immediately. He has to be starving. I devoured a sandwich in the kitchen, so I'm ready to catch a nap. I pull my chair next to his and tilt sideways, putting my head against his thickly-muscled bicep. This seems to do the trick, I figure I'll be asleep in minutes.

The deep rumble of Braxx's voice wakes me. I have no idea how long I napped, but at some point he'd pulled me so I'm sitting cross-wise on his lap, my head on his pec and his arms protectively around my waist.

"Sorry to wake you, Angel."

I open my eyes and try to wiggle off his lap. I'm so heavy I probably put his thighs to sleep. He holds me close. "Stay here, you looked so comfortable in that position."

I see Dr. Drayke is back in his hazmat suit, exiting the small operating room. "The surgery is complete. I've reviewed my scans, all radioactive material is gone. I just have to jettison the last piece."

"Will Axx be able to walk?" Braxx asks impatiently.

The doc himself looks paralyzed. Like a wind-up toy that quit walking in mid-step. He pauses a moment longer, obviously searching for a way to deliver some particularly bad news.

"One piece of shrapnel was lodged more deeply than our scans indicated. The bots did their job. It's just...the spinal cord was severed."

Warm tears gather behind my lids. I feel Braxx stiffen behind me.

"Could you...could you be wrong, doc?" Braxx's voice is rough with emotion.

"I can show you the scans. They're unambiguous. I'm sorry, Braxx. Completely severed," he pauses, I guess for us to begin to assimilate the information. "I've put him in an induced coma. I don't want him moving until the swelling goes down, that could exacerbate his condition.

"I suggest you talk to him. Although he's in a coma, research shows some part of his brain might hear you. Then get some real rest in your own bed. There's nothing you can do for him right now. His body has to recover."

Braxx lifts me off his lap and stands, twisting his head right and then left until it cracks. He moves toward Axx's room, then turns toward me when I don't follow.

"You're not coming in?" his muscles are slack. He looks tired and fearful.

"I figured you'd want to be alone with your gem."

"He needs me, Angel, and I need you."

Braxxus

These last two days have been interminable. I've tried to stay focused on caring for Axx as well as deepening my bond with Brie. We've both been so distracted and preoccupied, all we've done is eat, sleep and care for my brother.

I've watched Brie with Axx and can visualize her performing those same actions for me when I was in a coma only a few days ago. She's so tender with him, and thorough. She keeps him clean, moves his limbs, and maintains a steady stream of positive talk. She's massaging him right now.

"And when you're better, we're going to do some decorating in your room. You know, you just can't keep it so stark and functional. We'll have to put our heads together and think of something that pleases you.

"Is there a planet you've always wanted to visit?" she pauses as she rearranges the sheet that covers him to get access to his other leg. "I can tell what you're thinking, that the last planet didn't work out so well. But really, if you think about it, I think we've already encountered the worst-case scenario, it's been pre-disastered. There's nowhere to go but up…"

She just chatters on, talking about nothing, her voice soothing as her strong, competent hands slide along his skin and manipulate the muscles underneath.

Dr. Drayke enters and disconnects the intravenous tube that has been administering the med that's keeping Axx in a coma. "The drug should clear his system in an *hoara* or less. He'll probably be disoriented when he wakes." He snaps the rails up on both sides of the bed.

"He'll soon realize he's paralyzed. His mental state is as important as his physical state." He's behind Brie, who's leaning over, working on Axx's arm. He gives me a penetrating look, "We have to keep his spirits up."

Maybe it's the statement, or maybe the doleful expression on his face, but this highlights the severity of the prognosis. My stomach feels like it's falling through the floor when I realize with finality that my gem will never walk again.

Dr. Drayke leaves and Brie resumes her soothing chatter. I steeple my fingers in front of my face and try to come to terms with reality.

Axxios

Climbing up from sleep doesn't feel right. *Nothing* feels right. My head is foggy and my body's heavy. It takes a full *minima* for my eyelids to obey my command to open. When I do, Braxx and Brie are in front of me; their expressions confirm my suspicion that something is terribly amiss.

"What's wrong?" I ask, my throat dry and scratchy, my voice wavery as an adolescent male's.

Brie just shakes her head side to side, eyes widening.

"You were hurt when we were escaping the attack on Fairea," Braxx informs me. His eyes look up and to the right.

A secondary school student knows that's a clue someone's lying.

A shooting pain spikes from my shoulders down my back—I know he's not lying about me being hurt. I glance at Brie for confirmation, her eyes skitter from mine and she gets hard at work massaging my feet, presenting her back so I can't read her expression.

Realization dawns slowly—I can't feel a thing she's doing. I slide my gaze to my twin before I say, "that feels great, Brie."

Braxx's eyes round in surprise—he didn't expect me to feel anything.

Just to verify my suspicions, I try to move my toes. Nothing. Lift my knees. No. Wiggle my fingers? Yes.

"I'm paralyzed," I announce. I see my twin's muscles relax. Releasing a long sigh, he sags into the chair near my bed and grabs my hand.

"Gods Axx, I'm sorry."

"What happened?"

Braxx explains about the shrapnel, the radiation, and his difficult decision about whether to remove the metal or keep it in.

"You did the right thing." That's right, I instruct myself, stay focused on assuaging his emotions—don't get buried by your own. "The other choice sounds like certain death."

"I know, but I also knew you couldn't bear to be paralyzed." He raises the head of the bed one micron at a time, asking every *modicum* if I'm in any pain.

"I think the fact of the matter is, brother, that I'm feeling *no pain.*"

Gods, I wish that was true. My bottom half, no, more than half, feels heavy and like it's crawling with insects. My emotions are whirling inside, and for the last twenty years, I've had no practice dealing with them. But Braxx is feeling guilty, and if I can focus on relieving his pain, it will also relieve some of mine.

"The doc says this might be temporary," he explains, but his eyes dart up and to the right—lying again. "There's simply no way of knowing until the swelling goes down, and that could be weeks." He's nodding and for a moment I picture our mother making that exact same movement when she soothed us during the *Milagran* fever. Each and every day for weeks she nodded her head and told us it would all be better tomorrow.

Sly devil, Braxx. You really think you can lie to your gem? Although we didn't have our twinlink for an *annum*, did he forget it's working now? If I hadn't detected his lies in other ways, I could easily have felt it through our link.

"Sit, you two." I pat the bed for Brianna to sit, this will give her a reprieve from studiously avoiding me. I need to say this quickly before my emotions catch up with me. "I'm certain I'll be fine. If the doc says it might be a few weeks before I'm up and around and making you both miserable again, then so be it. Quit moping. When can I remove this undignified rag," I lift the neckline of my hospital gown, "and convalesce in our room?"

On the "our room" comment I spear Brie with a penetrating gaze. That was as close as I could come to an overt order for her to join us there. If my suspicions about the true status of my health are correct, the guilt I just loaded on her sealed the deal.

Dr. Drayke joins us and checks my vitals. I should ask to see the scans of my spine on his medpad, but I don't—the look on their faces confirms the truth. I need some time alone to figure out my next steps. I'm the gold. I do the difficult stuff. I always protected Braxx...and I always will.

Braxxus

Brie and I are getting Axx settled into bed in our cabin. I had a nagging feeling that something was wrong, things just didn't seem right. When I lift him up to transfer him from the gurney, my twinlink senses something is vastly wrong. He's hiding his emotions from me.

When we were teens and he'd been with a female, I discovered the hazy gray wall he projected when he was keeping a secret. I shouldn't be angry, I'm keeping things from him right now as well.

I should have known—he's taking this too well. My twin would never just listen to the news that he's paralyzed and then complain about his hospital gown. I'd rather hear him grumble, at least it would mean he's processing this. His silence is far worse.

Listen to him, talking to Brianna about what's for dinner like it's the most important thing on his mind.

"Whatever Maddie made, make sure you bring four portions back to our room," he instructs Brie. "Braxx still needs to put on some weight." He turns to me and casually asks, "Who's flying this thing, anyway?"

"Tyree's been sleeping on the bridge since we left Fairea. From what I hear, he did an admirable job getting us out of there in a hurry. We're somewhere in the Tallis sector. Savannah is manning our guns, Callista's on comms. Since we have nowhere we need to go right now, not a lot of money for fuel, and an inexperienced pilot at the helm, I thought it was a good plan to sit still until we know where we're bound for.

"Zar checks in with me daily, wants to know when I'll be ready to help. I was thinking, now that you're back among the living, that I might pull a shift tomorrow. Brie's offered to stay with you while I do that. I know Cally was looking around for some Cestus matches somewhere. Easy money, quick in and out, nothing to the death."

I'd like to get back to work. Not only would I be helping out, but it would throw Axx and Brie together, maybe help them connect.

"I'll be back in a few with the food," Brie announces, twirling her long hair around itself so it will stay out of her way.

As soon as the door closes behind her, the false smile vanishes from my face. "Cut the *drack*, Axx. Tell me what's going on?"

"*You* cut the *drack*, Braxx. Haven't you figured out yet that you can't lie to your twin?"

I sigh heavily. He's caught me, no use keeping up the charade. "I didn't know what to say. I just wanted to give you time for it to sink in a little at a time." I sit heavily on the chair at his bedside.

"Kind of puts a damper on the happily-ever-after-bondmates-with-your-angel thing, doesn't it?" he says.

"*Our* angel, gem. And why does this have to change things with her?"

He closes his eyes and shakes his head. I don't recall him ever looking so disgusted at me.

"She's a good female, that's why. She deserves a good life. She doesn't deserve to have to take care of an invalid all of her days, even if she gets one out of two healthy bondmates. And, let's be honest, she doesn't love me, Braxx. She doesn't even like me. This isn't a good match."

"That's not true. She said she likes you."

"When?" His blue eyes pierce mine. By his compressed lips and cocked eyebrow, I'm certain he knows the answer before I even say it. "After you got hurt," my voice is low. I sound ridiculous even to my own ears.

"Riiiight. She had a complete change of heart about an hour after I was almost pronounced dead. Quite believable, Braxx. I can feel the love emanating from her all the way down the hallway."

"She's taken care of you since you were injured, bathing you, massaging you, talking to you. Just like she did for me," I try to convince him.

"Sure. Because she's not a monster. Seriously? Is that geneslave still on board? I overheard he got hit with shrapnel, too. She's probably the one who's been feeding him. Because she's a nice person, Braxx. That doesn't mean she cares for him—or me."

"But she does."

"She cares for *you*, B. Notice the way she looks at you. Just for tonight. Look at that and then see if she looks at me the same way."

"She did, Axx. On Fairea, after that kiss, she was definitely looking at you like that."

"That's lust. We've always had...a connection. But that's over." He motions toward his cock under the covers. "I think the shrapnel killed any chance of that happening again."

The door rumbles against its jam, sounds like Brie's kicking it. I hurry to open it and help her in; her arms laden with enough food for six gladiators.

"Tonight's menu?" I ask lightly as I settle the tray on top of a dresser and begin to hand out the plates.

"It looks good and smells supremely edible," Brie announces. "Maddie calls it albast mignon and sliced nink in coquelle sauce."

I put a plate on Axx's lap, and Brie asks him, "Need some help?"

"It's my legs that don't work. My hands are fine. I believe I have the ability to adequately transport food to mouth," he snaps.

"Okay," her voice is small, the sound almost swallowed in her throat. "Sorry."

"Axx is in a shitty mood," I glare at him. "He should apologize."

"Absolutely," he agrees. "Not my best day, Brianna. My apologies."

Brianna

Well, that took my appetite away. My stomach is eating itself. Shit. Over the last few days, I've felt so close to Axx. First, there was that blistering kiss at the fair. Then I thought he was going to die. After that, I was caring for his beautiful body. There's nothing like taking care of someone on the verge of death to make you feel connected.

And now he has to wake up and be an asshole. I like him, I don't. I want him, I hate him. My emotions just aren't stable.

"I sat down in the dining hall to talk and had a bite with some friends," I lie. "I must have eaten more than I thought. I'm not hungry." I put my full plate on the dresser. "You guys are settled here. I think it's time for me to sleep in my own room."

They both try to convince me to stay, but I'm out the door and down the hall without even hearing their words.

Axxios

Braxx was so pissed at me he could barely stand to be in the same room with me while he shoveled food into his mouth. We were both relieved when Tyree called and asked for help on the bridge. I'm glad to be alone. I have a lot of thinking to do.

Thinking used to be easy, but now that I've found my bondmate, my emotions are swamping me. Yes, I admit to myself, she's my bondmate. It's ridiculous to deny it. I have all these warm and tender *dracking* feelings for her. I want to protect her, I want to sleep in the same room with her even if rutting isn't involved. My heart hurts when she's in pain.

And there's Braxx to think about. He's totally smitten, that's obvious. And I was right about the way she looks at him. She adores him. They laugh and have fun together. And then there's me. Wouldn't all three of us be better if I wasn't around?

My gem could get his mate. The female could get her male. They could all cry over my dead body and move on with their lives.

Part of me protests. Just because I can't walk doesn't mean I can't be productive. It's pretty easy to pilot a ship from a chair. I'm not certain I'm ready to be done with this second chance at life I've been given. But it's clear they'd both be happier without me—except Braxx's cock won't work without me around.

Chapter Thirteen

Brianna

I ran into Grace on my way back to my room. She's such a nice person, always checking in with everyone, wanting us all to be happy. She invites me to her cabin to talk. That's the last thing I want to do, so I ask her to play String Thing, her instrument, for me.

She plays beautifully, and there's something about her music that's so soothing. I could listen to her for hours. I'm surprised when her mate, Tyree, barges through the door. And by the look of things, he's pretty surprised to see me here as well.

"Who's driving this ship?" Grace asks, her fingers pausing over the strings in the middle of a song.

"Piloting, *amara*," he scolds amiably. "Braxxus is feeling well enough to help out. I didn't have to show him how to do anything. He says he learned on a ship of this class years ago." He spears her with a heated gaze. He's been piloting the ship alone for days. I imagine he practically ran here from the bridge, hoping to have some alone time with his mate, and here I am sucking the oxygen out of the room.

"I was just leaving," I say as I stand to go. A relieved expression flashes across Grace's pretty face.

I'm out of their room within seconds and speed-walking down the hallway before I hear any loud moans escaping from under their door. I know I should proceed straight to my room and enjoy some alone time. I haven't had a moment to myself since Fairea. But I don't perform a course correction when my feet head straight for the bridge. Braxxus will be there—alone.

His face lights up when he sees me slip through the doorway, then his eyes narrow in suspicion. "Angel. Everything all right?"

"Well, if you don't want company…"

"Of course I do. I want *your* company." He pats his lap. "Come sit with me."

"That won't be comfortable for you, I'll sit over—"

"My lap, Angel. Why wouldn't I be comfortable with you on my lap? You're warm and cuddly and maybe I could sneak a couple of kisses."

Braxx is changing, he wouldn't have been so forward a few days ago. I think I like it. I override my concerns about squishing him and slide gently onto his lap.

Instead of making an immediate move on me and initiating a makeout session, he settles me in a position facing forward, his hands respectfully on my waist.

"I love being on a ship, Angel," his breath rustles my hair. "It's so peaceful out there."

I look ahead and see the vast expanse of space in front of us. The diamond stars are strewn in the black sky. It goes on forever. There's a purplish nebula off to our right, and dazzling twin suns far to our left. Every muscle in my body relaxes as we sit in comfortable silence.

I was happy in my life on Earth. At least I thought I was. I loved my job, and it paid well enough for a decent apartment in Denver. I had good friends, went to concerts and loved exploring the mountains when I had time.

I know I'm only in my twenties, but I'd given up on men, at least for a while. That old expression about finding a man is true: the odds are good, but the goods are odd.

With online apps, getting dates was never a problem. Finding a decent man? Not so much. And here I am, snuggled in Braxx's lap. He's attracted to me, I'm not imagining that. At first, I discounted his attraction. I attributed it to the painting on his ceiling he was obsessed with. I thought he wasn't really crazy about me, he was crazy about some angel he'd been fantasizing about his whole life. Even him calling me Angel used to hurt my feelings because I felt like I wasn't really Brie to him.

But I don't believe that anymore. We've developed a real relationship. I like him in his many moods. I get a kick out of his goofy rain man side. I really appreciate how much he loves his brother—that shows character. And the few times he's allowed me to see his passion, yeah, that was pretty amazing.

I search myself, trying to see if I miss my old life. If we got a transmission from Earth that invited us back into our old lives with no questions asked, would I take it?

I gaze out the expanse of windows that ring most of the bullet-shaped room. Would I give this up? Braxx's muscular legs are under me, his hard chest behind me, his hands resting at my waist. I realize I don't want to let this go. That's reassuring and frightening at the same time.

"And all along I thought you were a man of your word," I tease in an attempt to bring myself back to the here and now.

"What?" His muscles tense. Obviously, my joke didn't strike him as funny.

"Kisses were promised but not delivered," my tone is breathy.

"I've always been a silver, Brie. This is new. Let's see if I can adjust."

He pierces me with a molten look, then lifts me as if I weigh no more than a pillow, turns me toward him, and straddles me over his lap, my knees tucked between his hips and the wide arms of the chair. Whoa, that ups the heat factor by a thousand! My core is riding a long, hard ridge that's bulging under his jumpsuit.

His hands lodge in my hair as he slowly lowers his lips to mine. "Brie," he says my name like it's the most important syllable in the universe, then kisses me soft and sweet for a moment. His lips graze mine, gentle as a whisper. Moving his head from side to side, he brushes me so tenderly it almost tickles. My hands explore his granite-hard muscles from shoulder to elbow, memorizing his contours while I admire his strength.

I can feel him shifting gears as his fists tighten in my hair. His kisses are harder, more insistent. He licks the seam of my lips, demanding entry. His tongue invades tentatively at first, then more forcefully. I assess the taste of him. It's less of a taste, more the feeling of a mountain meadow on a sunny summer day.

I'm focused on the intricate twining of our tongues and the way every cell in my body is awake and alive in a new way. His tongue is plundering my mouth even as one hand moves to my ass and presses me closer. For a second, my eyes fly open in surprise. This move is so sensual, so forceful. My core is riding the steel rod of his cock, and even through layers of clothes, I can feel his warmth, as I'm sure he can feel mine.

His tongue has pillaged my mouth so vigorously, it's all I can do to just hang on and enjoy the ride. I grab his shoulders and pull myself closer; the hard tips of my breasts press against his muscular chest. After stroking my tongue with his, he flicks the sensitive ridges on the roof of my mouth.

His hands glide from my ass to my shoulders and back. When those big, strong hands lodge on my ass again, he presses my core to him and thrusts. His passion is so ramped up, mine responds in kind.

His tongue retreats and he scrapes my lips with his teeth. A moan escapes my mouth. I'm on sensory overload. His hands and lips and tongue, riding his cock—it's almost too much. But it's also not enough.

"I've wanted to do this since the moment I met you, Brie. If you don't want this, you'd better say so now," his voice is so deep it's almost a growl.

My answer is to unzip his jumpsuit, pull it down over his shoulders and scrape my teeth across the silver skin of his shoulder.

I'm barely aware that he's pulling my t-shirt over my head until he tosses it to the floor.

"You're so b...Brie." Sweet man, even in the heat of passion he's trying not to use my most hated word. "Take off that contraption," he commands after spending no more than two seconds trying to figure out my bra.

I look at him after my bra joins its companions on the floor. His lids lower as he sucks in a breath. "I'm going to say it, Brie. You are so *dracking* beautiful I could forget to eat or sleep and just look at you all day. Don't forbid me from saying how lovely you are." He rests the weight of my breasts in the palms of his hands. "Wars could be fought over these."

He slows his pace, as if he doesn't want to frighten me with the intensity of his arousal. He drops a soft kiss on my collarbone, then draws the slowest line with his tongue down my skin to the rise of my breast, to the areola, and then my nipple. He licks the tip and I reward him with a soft moan and a hard thrust of my hips.

He sucks me into his mouth with a deep groan, then flicks up and down with his tongue so swift and hard and perfect I think I'll die. My clit is throbbing, pulsing in time with my heartbeat. My core is clenching and has to be dripping for him.

"Braxx," is all the words I can muster as I writhe rhythmically on his cock.

He finally releases one breast and attacks the other, giving it the same treatment. In the past, this has been enjoyable foreplay, but with Braxx, the pleasure is transcendent. Need is growing in my belly—and below. I don't just want release, I require it. I feel primitive, I'm riding his cock more quickly, grinding harder.

He nips the tip of my breast with his teeth, which creates a burst of pleasure that zings from that spot to my clit.

"Fuck!" escapes my lips. Dear God, that felt so good. He does it again, over and over, his silver head bobbing from his efforts.

I lean over and kiss him everywhere I can reach: the tip of an ear, the top of his head, the side of his throat. Now I bite the cords of his neck, his shoulder, his shiny silver bicep. I'm wild now. I just need more, I need it all. I'm pulling at his clothes. I have no intention of struggling to get that blue jumpsuit all the way off him, just low enough to pull out his beautiful cock.

Oh my God, I've finally got it in my hand. That gorgeous, silver, pulsing staff. It's so thick my fingers can't wrap around it. His sexy groan of pleasure, a moan from deep in the back of his throat, amps me up.

I have one hand around it and the flat of my other palm against the top. I can feel the slickness of his liquid as I trace circles with my hand on the head of his cock. I'm desperate for the taste of him. I scoot back toward his knees, then scramble off him, my knees on the floor between his feet.

I look up at him. This is his first time with a woman, I want to make sure he doesn't feel like I'm attacking him. I want this to be good for him. His head is pressed against the back of the chair, eyes shuttered closed. Oh, I don't think he's finding this objectionable in the slightest.

I lean over and breathe warmly on him, watching as he lifts out of his seat, wanting to press himself into my mouth. Nope, I'm in charge here, buddy, at least for a moment until the tables are turned.

Breathing hotly on him again, I make certain I've got his full attention, then use the flat of my tongue to gather the drops of his fluid and taste him. God, he tastes good—sweet. This feels intimate and connected and profound.

I swirl my tongue around the head, first one way and then the other until he's pumping toward me and groaning in pleasure. I prolong his wait a moment more, until the tone of his voice gets even deeper, gruffer, then I pull just the head into the warmth of my mouth.

He quits thrusting. When I open my eyes I see his hands clutching the arms of the chair so firmly it's a wonder something doesn't break. He's panting shallowly, mouth open. His obvious appreciation makes me want to please him even more.

I grasp the base of his cock with my hand and slowly take him deeper into my mouth.

"Brie," it's a breathy command.

I begin my game, advance and retreat. All the while I add to his pleasure with my hand at the base of his cock. My other hand slides between him and the chair to cup his heavy balls. He sucks in a shocked, delighted breath, then exhales in a heavy huff.

"Need to stop," he says as he tries to pull out. Somehow I know he wants to protect me from coming in my mouth. This only intensifies my desire to make him come, to taste all of him.

I quicken my pace, loving the taste of his flesh, the noises he's making, the pleasure I'm giving...and receiving. I'm drenched in my own fluids, my nipples tingle with desire, loving this connection.

And then I feel him spend. Hot jets of his release hit the back of my throat. His hands lodge on my shoulders, fingers biting a bit too hard because he's so lost in the bliss of his own orgasm. I'm thrilled by his abandoned, guttural bark of pleasure.

My head keeps bobbing, only slower now, trying to milk every ounce from him, and wring every drop of pleasure from his body. My tongue swirls languidly around his shaft, then focuses on the ridge, and finally licks the blunt head to catch every pearl of his fluid. Finally, reluctantly, I separate from him and sit back on my heels to take a mental picture.

His eyes are closed; he's breathing deeply as he savors the moment. Then his Caribbean blue eyes flare open and he bestows me with a look I know I'll remember until my dying day.

It's *that* look. Not the lust-filled looks I've seen before on just-fucked Earth males. But the look I've been waiting for all my life. The gentle, happy, longing of a male who wants me, who likes me, who...I stop myself—I'm not ready to even think the "L" word in the privacy of my mind.

"Is it a bad time to tell you again that I love you, Brianna? Does it cheapen things because you just gave me something precious that I've never had before? Would it make it better if I told you I will never want this with anyone else? Just you. Only you."

I scramble off my knees and onto his lap. Tucking my head under his chin, I take a moment to bask in what he just said. I don't want him to see my face. It would hurt him to see my disbelief. I need a moment to catch up to the emotions swirling inside me.

"Not a bad time, Braxx. I just need a moment to let it sink in." It *is* sinking in. And it feels amazing.

"I hope I didn't keep you at the helm too long," Tyree's voice interrupts through the overhead comm. "I'll be there in two *minimas*."

"*Drack*! I want to please you too, Brie," Braxx growls. He sets my feet on the floor and swiftly grabs our clothes, hands me mine and zips his jumpsuit in record time as I pull on my t-shirt and stuff my bra into my bottoms to save a moment. "

I'm certain we won't fool Tyree. All of these guys seem to have the uncanny ability to smell a woman's arousal at thirty paces. I have no doubt he'll smell sex before the bridge doors open.

"Sorry it took me so long," he strides in, hair still wet from a shower. "Hi again, Brianna." His eyes don't veer from mine, he isn't tossing me a lecherous look.

My already high estimation of Tyree just went up a notch. He has to know what we've been doing in here, but he's acting nonchalant about it. I guess it doesn't matter, we all know what he and Grace were up to, also.

The two males quickly set up a rotation schedule, with Tyree taking the lion's share—Braxx still isn't back to full strength.

We walk down the metal-walled hallway toward the cabin holding hands. I'm smiling like I just won the lottery. Which, in a way, I did. I feel like I won the prize.

"Come back to my room, Brie. Stay with Axx and me. We were meant to be together."

My feet quit moving forward. I've turned to heavy lead right here in the hallway. Did I just conclude I won the prize? What was I thinking? It's more like the booby prize. How did I just live through the last hour without giving one thought to the fact that Silver and Gold are a package deal? And the gold part of the package is an asshole.

"That nasty comment about not needing any help to eat...he just insulted the shit out of me."

"Yes, he did." He nods his head.

Good, don't gaslight me and tell me that Axxios wasn't just mean. "But today's the worst day of his life, Angel. He was just informed that he's never going to walk again. I think that would make anyone sour for at least an *hoara* or two."

Fuck you, Braxx, I think. *Fuck you for being right.*

I take a deep breath. "You're right. Definitely the worst day of his life. But Braxx, he and I are like oil and water on our best day. This threesome thing isn't going to work."

"Your culture is different. You have no role models. You've never seen a great tri-bond work, Brie. You admitted you like Axx. Unless you were lying." He spears me with a serious look, waiting for me to either confess I was lying or admit I like the golden boy.

Do I? Do I like him? I have to admit, he's mellowed since Braxx woke up. I can't judge him on today's performance. I'd be a bit testy, too, if the doc just told me I was paralyzed.

"I wasn't lying. It's just...there's a lot of history between us."

"Then let's make new memories," is his cheery reply.

I like Braxx far too much to throw this away right now. I have no options, really. How could I not go back to their room and see if there's a way to make this work?

Chapter Fourteen

Axxios

I hear them laughing as they approach the door. Great. As soon as they cross the threshold I can smell that they've been sexual. Even better.

Everyone on Mythros seemed happy in their tri-bonds. I never even wondered how people maintained their contentment with their bondmates. I'd assumed it would be effortless like with my parents and extended family.

I guess none of my role-models had an Earth female in the mix. Certainly none of them started out in captivity, forced to mate under the threat of death. And no bondmates I knew had a paraplegic male, dragging everyone down.

I want to say something cutting, so caustic in fact that they back right out of this room and set up house in her cabin. But I wouldn't do that to my twin. Gods, I love him so much and want him to be happy. I want her to be happy, too. I love her. I admit it. I'm just no good for either of them.

"Feeling better, Axx?" Braxx asks, a happy smile on his face.

How can I begrudge him his happiness? Less than two weeks ago he was dying, lying in a pool of his own urine. I'll bide my time. I'm certain the right path will soon become clear.

"Obviously you two must be feeling good." *Drack*, that was mean. How did I let that spiteful comment escape my mouth?

"Perhaps someone needs a nap?" he inquires pointedly, his eyebrow cocked.

"Sorry. Sorry to both of you. I have a lot to wrap my head around."

"All three of us are in uncharted territory," Braxx says. "Our parents never talked about how they got together, other than that it was arranged when they were young. Brianna and I probably shouldn't have done anything before we all discussed it."

He shoves a gust of apology at me through our twinlink even as Brie's head snaps back in disgust.

"Excuse me? We needed his permission before we…?"

"Not exactly permission, Brie," Braxx explains, "it's just that we're forging a new relationship and everything is new and fragile. We have three people's emotions to take into consideration. Doing something secretive, leaving someone out, could get things off on the wrong foot."

Brianna

He's right. As much as I might wish Braxx and I were a twosome, I've tacitly agreed that Axx is part of the package. I need to give this my best shot. Maybe Axx and I can repair some of what's broken between us.

I look at the golden twin, really look. God, he must feel awful. I've been self-absorbed. I've held a grudge. I don't think I'd be on my best behavior if the doc just told me I'd never walk again. How can I expect it of him?

I stride over to A's side of the bed, pull up a chair, grab his hand, and lean close to his handsome face. I take a deep breath and promise myself I'm not going to say one word that isn't true.

"You've done nothing wrong, Axx. Nothing." I pause a moment, slowly realizing that confessing my innermost feelings to him—to them both— is going to be harder than I thought. "How can anything good come out of what we were initially forced to endure? And yet...it did. I…" Shit, I don't want to say this. My stomach is clenching. Saying this will give him so much power over me. I gird myself; I literally throw back my shoulders and give myself a pep talk that I'm strong enough to handle this.

"I developed feelings for you, Axx." I take one deep breath, then another. "I've felt a deep attraction to you since, well, since the beginning. And I guess...it broke my heart that you didn't reciprocate. Yeah…" I nod, "it broke my heart."

My eyes are tearing, and I clench my jaw to gather control. I don't even glance at Braxxus, it's all I can do to keep looking at Axxios, reading his emotions—or trying to—his expression is shuttered. But he squeezes my hand, nice and tight. Is he trying to lend me some strength?

"I didn't really understand about the twinbond. Didn't have a clue about silvers and golds, seriously how could I know that? I knew you thought your brother was dead, but the extent of your love for him? The feeling of loss? How much that loss would affect your life? I had no way of understanding that. I couldn't fathom it.

"I felt rejected by you. You hurt my feelings. And the way to deal with it, to protect myself, was to get angry and reject you back. I...I think I'm still angry and hurt, but I'll get over that." I breathe deeper now, the worst is behind me. Besides, I'm focused on my hand in his golden one, I'm not looking into his beautiful blue eyes anymore.

"I really want to give things a try, Axx. And I want to help you. Even with all we've been through, you've always tried to be kind. I want to give back, to ease your burden." I take another deep breath and search my soul. I think I've said everything that needs to be said, at least for right now.

I gather the courage to look at him now. Whatever power I might have just given him, the damage is done.

His eyes are swimming with unshed tears. His jaw is tight, teeth clenched—I think he's trying to batten down his emotions. Somehow he pulls me into bed next to him, my back against his side, his arm tight around my waist. This reminds me of those days when we were slaves, when during the day we pretended that our masters were forcing us together, but during the night we experienced bliss in each others' arms.

He turns his head to whisper in my ear. "I hadn't experienced feelings, really felt them, since puberty, Angel."

My insides squeeze with a warm wave of pleasure when he calls me that.

"I wasn't aware then, but I'm fully aware now—I've loved you since the first day. I was too dense to feel it, maybe too stupid to understand it, but it's clear now how much I love you, Angel. It breaks my heart to know I hurt you. All I can do is say I'm sorry. I never want to hurt you again."

I climb gingerly over him to the middle of the bed, making sure not to even touch him during the maneuver. I spoon him, but before I throw my arm over his waist, I pat the bed behind me, indicating I want Braxx in bed with us, spooning me from behind.

Oh my God, this feels fantastic. I'm a Brianna sandwich. Peanut butter between silver and gold. Braxx snuggles me from behind, then speaks loud enough for both of us to hear, "I love you two. This is what I want. The tri-bond. Bondmates. For all of us to just love each other. If we do that, nothing else really matters. Besides, everything will work out, it always does."

Axxios

I'm glad I'm facing away. I can have a moment to process everything. It's like I'm two different people right now. Part of me is soaring in happiness. What just happened—Brianna saying she cares about me, feeling her arm tight around my chest, her breasts pressed against my back—it's what I've dreamed of since I was a child. That part of me is jubilant and wants to jump up and down in glee.

Which is the point. Because the other part of me knows with certainty that I'll never be able to do that. I'll never be able to run or jump, and possibly most importantly, I'll never be able to fulfill my Angel sexually again because I'm dead from the waist down.

Sadjoy. It's a Mythrian word I never understood...until today. I feel it now.

A fully-formed plan enters my head, just like that.

I'll love this female to the best of my ability. I'll love my gem in a way I haven't since I turned gold. I'll get on the Intergalactic Database every free minute to see what happens when the gold member of the tri-bond dies. Maybe there's a loophole. If I'm gone, gone for good, maybe Braxx's equipment will work when I'm not around. Then they can be happy without me. In the meantime, they'll never know I'm not truly part of their happy family.

Chapter Fifteen

Brianna

The stress of the past few days must have caught up with us. We slept yesterday from late afternoon straight through to this morning. I awaken, still sandwiched between my two guys. My two guys? How weird is that to say? But they are, and for right now, that feels mighty good. I give myself a swift little talking to, reminding myself that Axx is and might always remain a bit of an asshole. When he's sweet he more than makes up for it.

I had a friend who used to say, "Shit comes out of my mouth sometimes." He was right. We all mess up on occasion.

"Attention all males and females," Zar's stentorian voice interrupts over the shipwide comm, "this is a reminder that Shadow is making a special bake-a-cake for dessert tonight to celebrate the fact we all escaped Fairea with our lives. After that, don't forget the...let me check my notes...talent show that is planned.

"My beloved mate Anya wanted me to remind you that there is still time to put you on the program. She says, and I quote, 'be there or be square,' although I still have absolutely no idea what that means."

The comm clicks off and I feel both the guys stir next to me. Axx uses his arms to help him pivot toward me, Braxx is already looking my way. You'd think this would be awkward, waking up squished between both of them, but it feels divine.

"Do either of you have any hidden talents I should know about? Something you could display at a talent show?" I ask.

"I used to do intricate native dances from my world," Axxios informs me. "They would go on for *hoaras* to a steady drumbeat. I guess that's no longer an option," he intones solemnly, his face forlorn.

Braxx reaches over me and slaps his brother on the ass. "Wait," he says, then punches him on his shoulder, "that first one doesn't count, you couldn't feel it. Don't be an *oodvalt*."

I have no idea what an *oodvalt* is, but by its context and B's intonation, I assume it's the Mythrian equivalent of a jackass.

"Are you calling him a jackass?" I ask.

"I have no idea what a jackass is, but by your context and intonation, I assume it's the Earth equivalent of an *oodvalt*. My beloved twin never danced any intricate native dances." He whacks him again for good measure.

"And you, Braxx? Any hidden talents?" I ask over Axx's chuckle.

"I've been told I have artistic talent, but the only task I ever put it to was drawing pictures of one beautiful, alluring, mystical, heavenly angel. I don't think it could properly be displayed to our fellow shipmates."

"If we're going to try to do this bondmate thing, we've got to set up some rules. And rule number one is to avoid the 'b' word," I order sweetly.

"All in favor of avoiding the 'b' word say yes," Axx says, his voice happy and upbeat.

"Yes," I chime, but I'm outvoted. "It will never be fair, being one female to two males. I'll always be outvoted. I think either I should get two votes or you guys should each get half."

"All in favor of making this completely unfair and giving one person two votes say yes," Axx says.

"Yes."

"You're outvoted!" they say at the same time.

"*Drack* you!" I pout.

"All in favor of punishing Brie for using foul language say yes," Braxx says, and his voice has that husky quality that sends a little zing to my nether regions.

"Yes," they both say in unison, their voices deep and sexy. Both of them are looking at me like I'm little red riding hood and they're big bad wolves. Oh my God, I never realized my core would lubricate at the word "punishment." I guess I've got a lot to learn.

"I know the perfect punishment, Brianna," Axx says in a low growl. *Oh Grandma, what big teeth you have.*

"What is it?" I squeak.

"Braxx and I are going to give you intense pleasure for ten *minimas*, then leave you wanting. You get to marinate in that all day until after the talent show. Actually, I think my gem and I have a talent after all. But it's not for public consumption. We'll display it tonight, alone, in this room, for your enjoyment only."

I close my eyes and my breath releases with a huff. My clit is quivering already. "Ten minutes?" Does that sound like heaven, or hell? I have no idea.

"It will be eleven if you say one more word in argument. And you're forbidden from sexual release without our permission," my silver lover says from behind me. When did he change from being the nice one?

Axx pulls me toward him with a strong arm and with no preamble invades my mouth with his tongue. I'm not arguing. He licks the palm of his hand and circles my nipple with it, then plucks.

"Oh," is all I can say as I sink into a haze of sexual desire.

Braxx nips my neck from behind, then leans over and licks my nipple just as his brother is working the other.

"Too much," I manage to mumble. I'm not thinking straight. I look down and see both of their heads working my breasts. One golden, one silver. I wasn't lying, this *is* too much. I'll never be able to bear it. Not for ten minutes, not even for two more.

Braxx lifts his head to say, "You complained, Angel. Now it's eleven. Computer, eleven-minute timer."

I want to tell him that's unfair, that he should have started the timer at least two minutes ago, but I know he'll just add another minute to this delicious punishment.

Braxx moves down my body, nibbling and licking along the way until he arrives at the junction of thigh and torso. He nips me there until I writhe, trying to get his mouth and tongue to my core.

"Lie still," he commands, then redoubles his attention to the spot that delivers a delicious combination of arousal and urgency.

"I can't," my voice is a breathy whine.

"Computer," Braxx says, "add one minute to timer."

The word "fuck" almost escapes my mouth, but I know I can't tolerate even one extra minute of this sweet torture, so I bite it back.

Braxx slides between my legs, widens my thighs, and shoulders himself farther until he's up close and personal. He breathes hotly on my clit and all of my attention focuses there. Except I'm swooning under Axx's attentions, his fingers on first one nipple and then the other. His tongue pillaging my mouth, leaving me almost breathless with desire.

I'm incapable of thought. I can only feel. I'm swimming in a warm pool of lust.

Braxx has my legs split wide and dips his tongue into me, penetrating me as far as it can reach. A mighty bold step for a male's first exploration. He presses, licks, then laps my cream.

"*Drack*, Brie," he rumbles against my clit. "Gods, you taste divine."

The tip of his tongue gently touches my clit. I hazily wonder if he's getting acclimated. Then he flicks it harder, touching, pressing and lapping almost as if he's making sure to touch all the numbers on an imaginary clock face. By the second rotation, he's magically found nine o'clock, my happy spot. I must have given away the secret by the deep moan that escaped my lips at the same time my hips levitated off the bed.

"That's right, gem," Axx pulls away just long enough to praise his brother, "make her moan."

Braxx keeps his lascivious attentions on the right spot until I'm writhing on the bed.

"You know she's close when her moans come from deep in the back of her throat like that," Axx praises.

I can't take any more. The urge to come isn't sneaking up, it's barreling down on me. No, no, no, I'm screaming in my mind when Braxx slides a finger inside me. No, I can't control myself. He can't keep doing that without making me fly apart.

Another finger joins the first. So not fair. Is this what it's going to be like forever? Two against one? That thought alone almost puts me over the edge.

Axx knows every one of my tells. He has to recognize I'm two seconds from release, because his hand snakes down and cups my mons, his fingers blocking my entrance from his brother. He croons in my ear, "It's okay, little Angel. We won't punish you any further."

I'm still panting, heart racing, clit thrumming. Braxx slides up and plays tenderly with my hair while Axx applies the gentlest pressure down below, helping me get control. The computer announces the timer is up. It will take me all day to recover from this.

Axx bites along my jawline from ear to chin. "It's going to be a long day for you, Brie. You know you're forbidden from taking care of yourself, right?"

I'm still so deep in a lust-induced haze it takes a moment to understand his meaning. "Yes." I nod.

"Braxx and I will apply the antidote tonight," he promises huskily.

Fuck you, I tell them in the privacy of my mind. But crap, that was the most sensual thing I've ever experienced. Maybe this bondmate thing might be the best thing that's ever happened to me.

Axxios

Bittersweet. Is that what the rest of my life is going to be like? What happened in our bed this morning was one of the best moments of my life. Being with my gem, knowing we're with our bondmate, and working together to pleasure the female we love? That was what life should be about.

And at the same time, not being able to feel anything below the waist? Certainly there must be a word more crushing than despair. How crazy that half the time I was focused on giving Brie pleasure and the other I was wallowing in my own misery

Enough of this, it's getting me nowhere. I've got research to do. I need to find out if a silver is capable of an erection after his gold dies.

Braxxus

My twinlink with Axx is a blessing and a curse. It was so good finally having our twinlink again. Although I knew I missed him, I don't think I'd realized just how much until we reconnected.

But I can perceive his emotions almost as if they're my own. He thinks he's graying them out, hiding them in the shadows of his mind, but I feel them.

He wasn't fully there in bed with Brie and me this morning. He's disconnected. He laughed and joked with us today, but he's not happy. Then again, how could he be? He's paralyzed.

After Brie left I helped him with his shower. I had to turn away as I carried him there and placed him on the shower chair we grabbed from medbay. I didn't want him to see the pinched anguish on my face, to know my heart was breaking for him. He's lost so much.

I guess we're both hiding things from each other—or trying to.

I was missing a piece of the puzzle when it suddenly strikes me. He's contemplating suicide. The thought pierces into my brain in a *modicum*, but I'm certain it's true. That would explain his near nonchalance about his paralysis as well as the thick curtain he's erected between us.

I can't talk to him, he'll just deny it. If what happened in bed today can't convince him how sweet our life can be, even with his challenges, I don't know what could.

I grab the computer pad and start feverishly paging through the Intergalactic Database. I have an idea.

Brianna

Shit. I read somewhere that the female equivalent of blue balls is called heavy pelvis. Boy is my pelvis heavy.

I'm walking to the dining room for breakfast and can't keep my finger from sliding along my lips, almost as if I can replay what just happened in my bed. Well, it's not my bed. Or...maybe it is? I don't understand exactly what the status of our relationship is. Bondmates? Not quite? Is there some ceremony we have to go through? Do I really want this?

I'm the type of girl who likes to quantify things. Yep, I like to have things nicely tied down, yet nothing seems settled at all. And right now the thought of tying things down gets me hornier because all of a sudden, after my little punishment in bed this morning, the picture of being tied down just flew across my internal vid screen.

This is wonderful and exciting and scary all at once. After grabbing some breakfast, I'm going to head for my room, take a shower, and try like hell to resist the urge to break the twins' "no release" rule.

Chapter Sixteen

Axxios

I'm sitting in the small chair in the corner of our cabin, already dressed in my black-leather gladiator regalia. That was a new lesson in humility—having my twin *dracking* dress me. It seems every *hoara* brings a new revelation of the indignities I'll be subjected to if I choose to stay in this life.

Then I watch Brie and Braxx. What a great couple they make. Of course, I'd never really seen a couple on Mythros, my only role models were triads. But on the ship, the couples who are paired off look cute and happy.

But I'm not certain how cute and happy these two can remain if my brother can't get it up for his bride.

And where that leaves me? Nowhere. I found nothing in the Intergalactic Database that spoke to the issue of silvers getting erections after their gold is dead.

I have one more idea, but I've put it off for tomorrow. I just didn't have the stomach for it. I could contact Dr. Merendi back home. He was our family physician. He treated Braxx and me for childhood illnesses as well as the occasional broken bone.

If he doesn't know the answer to my question, he'll be able to find it. The problem is that my fathers will be fully briefed on my condition and whereabouts within a *minima* of the communication.

We overthrew our masters more than two months ago. I've had ample opportunity to contact them since then. I've chosen not to. My parents were always hard on me. I think we all knew on some level that I'd be the golden twin. Even before the change, I was charged with protecting my gem.

I knew they'd blame me for his death even though I was piloting my own ship at the time. Now that he's alive, I gave some thought to a quick trip to Mythros to see the family. It didn't appeal. I assumed Braxx would ask to go at some point, but I think first his Angel and now his twin have been at the top of his priority list, not our parents.

With this paralysis, I can visualize in detail what our reception will be. I can imagine them giving Braxx *drack* for not protecting me—even though that's ridiculous. And I'm certain B knows as well as I do that bringing a human home to meet the parents will not thrill any of them.

It would be nice to spare all of us that drama.

But I may have to call Dr. Merendi tomorrow. I'll do anything to make the cute couple standing in front of me happy.

"You two look fantastic. I had no idea talent shows were a gala affair," I tell them brightly. Braxx is dressed in an outfit matching mine. His back is covered in clear plas-film under the black leather sash, as is mine.

Brie's wearing a simple pink dress she borrowed from Grace for the occasion. It's not fancy in the slightest, but except for the Mirasian silk she wore to the *dracking* fair, I've never seen her in anything but leggings and the shapeless, baggy top she calls a t-shirt.

She smiles shyly. Someday I'd love for her to know—really know down to the depths of her soul—how beautiful she is. Perhaps it will take more time. Nothing else has worked.

There's a knock on our cabin door and Braxx looks like he just got caught filching money from our mother's purse. I only have a moment to wonder what he's hiding before he throws the door open and invites whoever's out in the hall inside.

Dax carries in a three-*fierto* tall contraption. Both males are beaming. By her expression, it's clear Brianna's not in on the little secret—nor am I.

"See you in an *hoara*," Dax says as he hurries out.

"An exoskeleton, Axx!" Braxx grabs the computerized walking device, comes over and clasps me on the shoulder. "I've been designing it and producing it on the 3D printer all day. Let's get you walking."

Setting it in front of me, he maneuvers my legs into it. It's compact, with little more than two sturdy rods that hug the contours of the outside of each leg. The rods connect around the back of the waist. That and a wrist controller are all I need.

I stand and almost fall. I need to figure out my center of gravity. B is patient with me, letting me lean most of my weight on his shoulder until I get the hang of it. In less than five *minimas* I manage to quickly pace from the door to the back wall and return.

As soon as I can shamble on my own, I let go of B's shoulder and do a few more laps. On my own. Now that I feel moderately competent, I take a moment to glance at Brie.

She's given me room to practice with the gizmo, and is standing just inside the bathroom threshold. Her smile shows a combination of pride and joy. "I'm so happy for you, Axx. How does it feel?"

"I never knew how good standing and walking felt until I was relegated to a chair for the past few days. Being able to look at my gem eye to eye again—that's amazing."

I'm smiling. Not only can I walk, I feel like I can fly. A weight has been lifted off me. And look at my bondmates. Braxx pulled Brianna into the room and has his arm around her waist. They're both so happy for me. This is what I've wanted all my life.

I've quit paying attention to my legs and movement, and almost stumble, but I right myself. Can I do this? Can I allow myself to remain here and let these two love me? I don't know how I'll feel tomorrow. I just know that right now I think I might be able to stay.

Brianna

I love these guys. Those are the only words coursing through my thoughts. I'm choked up and hot tears are welling in my eyes. I love Braxx, he's so easy to love. And I love Axx, too. He's got more layers than his twin, but that's not necessarily a bad thing.

Somehow I maneuver us into a tight circle and force a group hug. It's so good to look up at Axx again. Oh, the way he's looking at me, like he could administer the antidote he promised me right this minute, I actually feel weak in the knees.

"Maybe we could skip the talent show?" I wheedle. "There are twenty-two other people on board. I doubt they'll miss the chubby girl and the handsome twins."

Whoa. By the expression on both their faces, you'd think I just said their mother looked like a baboon. Axx's face turns to golden thunder. Braxx's turns to lightning.

"Come here," Axx orders as he pulls me into the bathroom.

The three of us stand in front of the mirror above the sink. Their faces are so serious, a little thought pricks the back of my mind that they're planning a punishment I might not like.

"Tell me what you see," Braxx instructs. Both of them are looking at me through our reflection in the mirror, and by the looks of things, they wish they could shoot lasers out of their eyes.

"Two handsome guys," my voice quivers, "and me."

The corners of their mouths slash down even further as my eyes flick from one to the other.

"More," Axx dictates.

"Two huge, muscled Mythrian males, one silver and one gold. Dressed up for a night on the town—gladiator style. Turquoise eyes, chiseled cheekbones, masculine lips. Nice hair?" I end on a question, hoping I've passed the test.

"And the person in the middle?" Braxx asks.

"Describe her," Axx commands.

Well crap. I was avoiding that. I'm usually so good at not seeing my own reflection.

"Dark brown hair, green eyes, pink dress." There. That should do it. I look up at Braxx, usually the softer of the two, hoping the quiz is over.

"Stop it, Brie. Don't make light of this," he says, his face still tight with anger.

If *his* face is this irritated, I don't want to spare a glance at his tougher, angrier brother.

I look into the mirror, trying to see what they want me to see. I don't know what they're fishing for.

"Brown hair," I repeat, "green eyes. Freckles?" Is that what they want?

Braxx looks furious. I've never seen him this angry, even when they told him his gem would never walk again. It's Axxios whose face has softened. He stands behind me, gently resting his hands on my shoulders.

"Try this, Angel. Look into my eyes in the mirror." He pauses. "Really look, that's right." His voice is sensitive and tender. That's the voice you could hold onto during a rough patch. It's full of warm affection.

"Good job. What do you see?"

The river of time seems to stop flowing. I know this is serious. I consciously unclench every muscle in my body and try to breathe easy. My shoulders relax, my jaw slackens and I lose myself in his gaze.

"That's right, Angel, tell me what you see in my eyes. Only my eyes."

"Love?" The awareness hits me like an avalanche. "Love, Axx. I see so much love. Oh my God. So much." A liquid warmth suffuses my chest as I allow myself to receive it.

"That's right. Now look at Braxx's eyes in the mirror. What do you see?"

Somehow I gather the nerve to look—all the fury is gone from his gaze. I see him regarding me with so much affection I feel lightheaded. It's penetrating me and moving through me like a wave of warm, passionate energy. It's so intense it could be overwhelming, but it's not.

"What do you see?" Braxx prompts gently.

"Love. You guys love me." I'm full-on crying now, my lips are quivering and I can't take my eyes off the mirror as my gaze bounces from one pair of compassionate blue eyes to the other.

"Now," Axx says. "Imagine you're looking through our eyes and look at yourself. Describe yourself."

It's the bravest thing I've ever done to tear my eyes from his and look at myself. My image wavers before my eyes, then crystallizes.

I take a long moment to allow the emotions swirling inside me to register with my brain. When I look at myself through their eyes, everything changes. Like getting a new pair of glasses, everything looks different.

"I see Brianna." I breathe deeply. "Cute upturned nose, intelligent green eyes, they're inquisitive. I see a perfect mouth, just made for smiling...and kissing. I see a graceful neck, the ideal smattering of freckles, and look...," I pause and look first to one twin and then the other. "Dear God, I look just like I belong with both of you."

I know they're smiling down at me, and I want to look at them right now, I do. But first my lids slam closed and I just savor this moment. For the first time in my life I feel totally at home in this body. This is my body and I fully inhabit it. I belong here, dammit, and nothing needs to change. I'm fine exactly as I am.

I have to say that out loud, right this minute, "I'm fine exactly as I am." Then louder, "I'm fine exactly as I am."

And I realize my guys are chanting it now, "You're fine exactly as you are, Angel."

They bend down and envelop me in a three-way hug that touches my heart, and my soul.

"We belong together, Angel." Axx captures my chin in his hand and lifts my face until I'm looking at him. "We're a beautiful triad. We're going to make it through all of this together."

His voice still sounds so serious. I wonder if he's reassuring himself as well as me.

"Speaking of three's..." Axx steps behind me and turns me toward the mirror. "Close your eyes." He reaches over my head, then I feel him place a necklace around my neck. I'm already smiling. I know exactly what it is.

"Open your eyes," Braxx urges.

It's the necklace he showed me on Fairea. My hand flies to it. I adore the feel of it, the fact that it's already warming from my body heat, and that it symbolizes our tri-bond. I'm torn between holding it and letting go so I can get a good picture of what it looks like on my skin.

"I love it. It's the perfect symbol for our tri-bond—gold for Axx, silver for Braxx and pink rose gold for me." I'll admit it, I'm tearing up.

I glance up at them both, they're looking at me with love and admiration. My stomach does a happy flip.

"But you've still got to sit through an entire talent show before we administer your antidote," Braxx jokes, a sexy smile slashing across his face.

And then he's kissing me. Not soft, tentative kisses, but hard, claiming ones. The kind of kisses that usually accompany a good fucking. But he's barely touching me anywhere except my shoulders. He's pulling me close and kissing the shit out of me like he owns me.

My response is not to push him away. My core responds with warm approval in the form of clenching and copious amounts of lubrication.

"Braxx, we have to leave soon," my words protest, but I press myself so close to him daylight couldn't peep through. My heel has snaked behind his knee, pulling him closer.

"Right you are, Angel," Axx agrees, his voice soft and soothing even as he sweeps my hair off the back of my neck and nibbles behind my ear.

He's known my secret spot for ages and loves to use it against me. I'm panting even as I move my hands to Braxx's magnificent ass and pull him against me so hard I can ride his cock through the stiff black leather that protects it.

They must have communicated through their twinlink, because they both kiss me once more—a bit too chastely for my taste—and stand up to their full height.

"We should go," Axx says forcefully, even as he's apologizing with his gaze.

Axxios

The sheer joy of being able to walk to the dining hall on my own power is surpassed only by the pride of having my little family with me. Brie's in the middle, exactly where she should be, and Braxx is on her other side. We're all walking in step, talking excitedly with each other, as if there's only the future ahead of us. As if Braxx and I hadn't both almost died within the last lunar cycle. As if I wasn't damaged beyond repair.

We arrive a few minutes before the show is to start. Stryker smiles and nods at me. Dax's impossibly deep voice booms out, "Good to see you walking again, Axxios." Maddie gives me a long hug, then asks if she can bring me a snack.

I receive a few happy waves and many more congratulatory comments. Everyone on board is genuinely glad for my good fortune. I don't think it's all about the fact I walked in here on my own power, they're all happy to see the three of us together and holding hands.

We take our seats a moment before the talent show starts. I grab three seats in the back row to give us privacy.

I've never been to a talent show before. Are they all like this? It's interminable. There are some entertaining moments. Grace's melodic music was lovely as usual. Petra performed an interesting gymnastic routine while wearing clothes that covered her from ankle to neckline. I'm certain her "costume" was designed by Shadow, her protective mate.

And who knew huge Dax of all males would recite the most sensitive love poem ever written by a member of his race? His entire performance was executed while gazing deeply into Dahlia's eyes with utmost sincerity.

B and I each held one of Brie's hands during his poetic recitation. I could tell she was getting choked up. If I was still a complete male, my cock would be hard as *mamnite*. I love that Brie gets emotional about Braxx and me.

I consult my heart. I've always had an intense bond with my gem, many who knew us remarked on how close we've always been. And Brie? I would have given my life for her since the day I met her, and that was before my emotions returned from where they were buried for decades. Now I love her. I would do anything to keep her from pain—either physical or emotional.

Have I really decided to stay in this triad? Have I transformed from a male who was ready to take my leave of this lifetime to being willing to stay? All in the span of a handful of *hoaras*?

Gathering my emotions in check, I wonder what it's going to feel like to watch my silver take the lead in the bedroom tonight. I'll be sidelined—able to bestow a few kisses, assist with a finger or a tongue, but will have to watch my brother conduct the "big finish." I can only imagine how completely that will decimate any shred of ego I might have left. By the way my heart is squeezing inside my chest, I wonder if I might call Dr. Merendi tomorrow after all.

I try to pay attention to the show. Other than Grace and Petra, who have true talent, I realize we're watching one gladiator after another get up on stage and "perform." The idea of talent seems to be optional for the males—and they all seem to be having a great time.

I wonder what it is about planet Earth that none of the women are willing to be dragged up on stage.

"No!" Maddie screams when Stryker attempts to get her to join him for a song that could cause a healthy person's ears to bleed.

"Why don't any of the females want to have fun?" I whisper to Brie.

"Because it's not 'fun' to feel like a fool," she whispers back.

"But no one's a fool, Brie. It's just a good time."

"Not for us. On Earth there's a difference between having fun and being made fun of."

I squeeze her hand to show support, even though it's hard to understand the females' reluctance to play. I wonder if there's something in their culture that contributes to this, and if it's the same thing that makes my angel so self-conscious about the way she looks.

My reassuring grasp on her hand turns sensual as I take one finger and circle it in her palm. She's so responsive, her mouth opens on the tiniest gasp as her eyes flash to mine. I point out what I'm doing to Braxx through our twinlink, and within *modicums*, he's mimicking my movements down to the same pace and direction in her other palm.

Within a *minima* I can smell Brie's arousal. I lean over, breathe hotly in her ear, and say, "I want you to sit on my face tonight." I don't take my eyes off Stryker who's up on the makeshift stage giving an exhibition on how to tie knots. Brie sucks in a breath as her scent blooms sweeter in the air.

I hear Braxx's deep whisper, "I want to hear the exact pitch of your scream when you come on my cock."

I feel her wiggle her hips in her seat.

"Sit still, Brianna. Don't break any rules or we'll have to punish you again."

She takes a breath, about to protest, then glances up at me and sees my authoritative gaze. Clamping her mouth shut, she closes her mouth and tightens every muscle in her body.

"Trying to be a good girl, Brie? Good girls are rewarded," my tone is full of promise.

"You do want a reward, don't you?" Braxx whispers to her.

She makes a slight strangled sound in the back of her throat and swallows.

Stopping the gentle circles I'm making on her soft palm, I reach up and slowly, sensually lift her long hair off her neck and lay it over her other shoulder. Even though we're in the back row of the audience and no one is looking, I act nonchalant as I trace my thumb in lazy circles on the back of her neck.

This spot is her weakness. I watch her eyelids flutter down for a long moment. Her jaw muscles clench even tighter. I can only imagine the muscles in her core clamping in on themselves as she tries to control her rising arousal.

Out of the corner of my eye I see her lean forward almost imperceptibly to press her sensitive bottom into the seat. I lean over, lick her earlobe and then the whorls inside her ear. She gasps quietly, then releases one soft pant, trying to maintain her composure. "You broke a rule, little Angel. You might want to give some thought to what you're willing to do to atone."

I've never before heard the sound that escapes her. It's a cross between a squeak and a strangled moan.

"Mercy, Axx. Please, let me get to our room before you make me spontaneously combust." She looks at me, her green eyes wide, pleading. I take pity on her and remove my hand from her neck to chastely grasp her hand. My silver, though, drags her hair to the other side of her neck, rests his elbow on the back of her chair, and slides his fingertips from the collar of her dress to her hairline.

"Braxx." I hear her hiss. "Please."

But his hand never ceases its lazy caress up and down, then left to right along the sensitive flesh of her neck.

Shadow's boring lecture about the history of Gaia grinds to a halt. He's been obsessed with it of late, believing the ancient

Gaians seeded all of our planets with their DNA and then let life evolve. He's convinced that's why most humanoid species throughout the galaxy have 98% common genetic material. He wants us to search farther into uncharted space looking for their planet of origin. He believes they're still there and will welcome us. Personally, I think this is delusional.

"Thank you, Shadow, that was very informative," Anya says. "How about one more round of applause for everyone who performed tonight?"

I'm not certain I can listen to one more word. I can't wait for me and my gem to slip my bondmate into bed. Tomorrow I might have mixed feelings about my future, but what tonight has in store? Of that, I have no doubt. My new mate will scream with pleasure until she begs for mercy. Many times.

Brianna

The three of us walked back to our wing hand in hand, just as we walked to the dining hall ninety minutes ago. However, as soon as we crossed the threshold of the double doors that separate our wing from the rest of the crew, everything changed.

The twins' mental bond must be getting stronger every day because they were coordinated down to the last second.

Braxx slid his hands from the outside of my knees up my dress to my waist, skimmed down my panties, and pulled them off of me at the same moment Axx pulled me up and straddled me open across his waist.

Axx strode right past our cabin doorway to the solarium at the end of the hall. I've only been in here once before, on cleanup day. This room is magical. It's bullet-shaped, with floor-to-ceiling windows on all sides except the wall with the entry door. Even the ceiling is a shallow dome comprised of windows.

Last time I was here I got distracted by the endless array of sparkling stars interspersed between purple-blue nebulae. Right now though, how could I pay attention to anything other than what the guys are doing to my body?

Braxx drags my dress over my head, struggles for less than ten seconds with my bra, then pulls out the knife he bought on Fairea which was attached to his belt. He doesn't activate the laser, just uses the sharp blade to cut the strap and pull it off me.

"*Drack*, Brie," he breathes into my ear. "The smell of your arousal almost made this silver rut you on that *dracking* stage."

"Touch her channel, Braxx," his brother suggests. "I bet she's dripping wet for us."

Braxx does just that and sucks in a harsh breath. He rides two fingers from my core to my clit and back again. He presses his chest against my back, pushing me even more tightly against his twin, then steps out of the way as Axx flattens me against one of the tall window panes.

The chill of the glass jolts me to a sharper level of consciousness. I open my heavy lids and look into Axx's eyes of piercing turquoise blue. I'm riding his waist, my legs straddling his hips. I'm only vaguely aware of the plastic exoskeleton struts notched under my thighs.

Braxx is to my side, his tongue biting the cords of my neck and his fingers plucking my nipples.

"Want to give her release here, gem?" Braxx asks, his impassioned voice like rough gravel.

"She was so naughty in the dining room, Braxx. I saw her rocking against the seat of her chair. Five more *minimas* in here." He tells his comm to set a five-minute timer, then, "Tease her little bud, gem."

Braxx's fingers leave one of my nipples, slide down my flank, between my thighs and immediately drive into my dripping channel from behind. When they've collected enough of my liquid, he paints my clit with it before gently circling it.

"Braxx, please," I'm begging, feeling no shame in the act, only desperation. I'm wiggling, writhing, trying to get his fingers to assuage my frenzied need. I smell my own arousal. I hear my little pants as if they're far off. I shutter my eyes, already on total overload.

He pulls his touch away, his fingers resting on my inner thigh. "Are you breaking rules again, Brie? We'll have to teach you to be still."

Axx's hands slide down and rest where the meat of my ass meets my thighs. His warm fingers are close enough to my wet heat to vie with his brother's for my attention.

I want to scream, I want to pummel Axx's plas-film-covered back, then scratch the bare skin of his flanks. I don't do that, I just kiss him, thrusting my tongue deep into his mouth. My prehistoric brain, the only part of my mind still capable of thought, is trying to distract me from the urgent need pulsing in my clit.

Braxx seems happy with my compliance, because his fingers slip back into me. They give me a modicum of relief even as they ramp my need higher.

"Let's get our Angel into our bed," Axx breathes, his voice so low and deep I almost don't comprehend his words.

"Yes, administer the antidote," his brother agrees as he deliberately pumps me once, twice, three times more and then retreats.

This wing is abandoned except for us. It's the work of a moment for us to quick-march back to our room, my core still pressed to Axx's belly. In less than a minute Axx has gently tumbled me onto the bed.

Braxx grabbed my clothes and has tossed them onto the dresser. He's already scrambled out of his regalia. Even in my lust-induced haze, I can't tear my eyes from him—he's so amazing to look at. The twins' features are identical, with aquiline noses, high cheekbones, and lips that demand to be kissed.

But to see him standing there, his thick cock jutting toward me, pulsing slightly with every heartbeat—it makes my mouth dry with desire. He's thinner than his gem. When he moves I can see every perfect muscle slide under his silver skin.

I feel that odd swirl of energy I experienced when the three of us were together on Fairea. It's pulsating and circling and building with each circuit. It must have something to do with the twinbond—no, maybe this is the tri-bond. It feels powerful and connected and somehow sweet at the same time. It's this moment, right here, that cements my thoughts that this union is perfect, maybe preordained. The three of us were meant to be together.

There's a dim thought in the back of my head calling to me, increasingly louder. It tells me I should be worried about what's going to happen next. Because in the next hour, every sex act that can be performed between two men and one woman is going to transpire.

I've given it enough thought to wonder if it will hurt. But these are my bondmates. Nothing is going to happen in this bed that won't be wonderful, I'm certain of that.

I glance over at Axxios and glimpse just a fraction of his expression before he schools his features into the bland appearance I've come to know is his hiding face. He's sitting on his chair, his exoskeleton removed and lying on the floor. The chair is too far from the bed for him to transfer on his own power.

He and his twin must be communicating through their link. Braxx's sensual I-want-to-get-down-to-business face has been replaced with his I-need-to-care-for-my-twin face. He hurries to his naked brother's side and lifts him onto the bed.

The moment has been doused with ice water. I can't read Axx's mind like his twin can, but I know as sure as I'm breathing that he's lost in despair. I imagine we're all thinking of what's missing at this moment instead of what we have.

Well, Braxx wasn't the only one who was busy today. I took a deep dive into the Intergalactic Database when I wasn't fantasizing about the "antidote" I was going to receive tonight.

As Braxx would say, *everything is going to work out*, at least if I have anything to say about it.

I wait until Braxx settles onto his side of the bed, then tell the computer to turn out the lights. For a moment I consider telling the guys about the scientific journals I read from all over the galaxy about erections after spinal cord injuries. That will be as sexy as Shadow's lecture about Gaia. I decide to just launch into action.

I straddle Axx, my dripping core against his ripped belly, then lean down to kiss him. All the alpha sexual energy he used to exude is gone. If I could see his face, I'd know for sure, but I'm pretty certain most of his attention isn't on me. His thoughts are probably on everything he lacks.

I keep kissing him, just lips on lips. I don't want to be the aggressor here—he needs to come back and join this party on his own.

"You promised me release, Axx. Apply the antidote." I keep riding him, pressing my core against him as I graze his chest with my pebbled nipples.

Axxios

If this triad is going to have half a chance of succeeding, I need to get my mind in this bed and stop thinking about contacting Dr. Merendi. *Drack* it. I've wallowed in self-pity long enough. I'm the gold, I do hard things, I don't give up, I don't settle for second best, nor do I give it.

I focus on this moment. My angel, the female I've known would be my bondmate since I was five years old, is in my arms. The room is bathed in the scent of her arousal, the sound of her desperate pants permeates the air. My gem is nearby, and although he's trying to keep his quiet thoughts out of my awareness, I know he's more than ready to plunge his cock into our mate. The only thing missing is me, and by all the Gods, I'm back and fully present in this room.

I grip Brie's shoulders as I invade her mouth with my tongue. She slips her hands behind my head and presses herself against me as if she can't get enough of my taste—as I can't get enough of hers. Her skin is warmer than I've ever felt it. She's burning for me—for us.

"Braxx and I will give you release when we're good and ready, little Angel," my voice is deep and breathy. My palms slide down her back and grab the cheeks of her ass, pressing her core against me even harder.

"Ride me, Brie," I order her as my hands work her against my pelvis. I can't feel anything below my waist, but I must be using just the right pressure because her breathing is louder now, and jagged. She sits upright on me, and increases the pressure she's using to grind her nub against my pubic bone.

I reach a finger behind her, between her cheeks to dip it inside her wet channel and my breath quickens with her sharp gasp of pleasure. She's panting and rotating her hips, trying to find relief.

"Join us, gem," I urge Braxx. He slides in behind her and cups her breasts in his palms, plucking her nipples. "Computer, lights on dim." I want to see this.

It's spectacular. Brie's skin is flushed reddish pink. Her chin is tilted toward the ceiling, her eyes closed. She's riding in a cocoon of pleasure so deep she's not even complaining about the lights. Braxx's hands are working her nipples, his cock pressed to her ass.

"Fuck her sweet pussy, gem," I say on a moan. Although my cock isn't working, my libido—the sexual thoughts in my head—are ramping up my enjoyment.

I help her lie forward on my chest, knowing her pink folds will be presented to my twin for both their pleasure. He leans forward and kisses her sweetly. She hooks my neck in the crook of her elbow, pulling me close to join their kiss.

"Are you ready, Angel?" Braxx asks.

"I've been ready all day."

I feel her thrust herself back, signaling her eagerness.

Braxxus

"I love you, Angel," I tell her as I slide the head of my cock along her slick folds.

"I love you, too, Braxx. I love you both."

I press into her warm tightness in one motion. Heaven. This must be what they talked about when they described heaven in temple back home. I stop moving for a moment and kiss her neck as I get acclimated to the firm warmth squeezing my cock. I've dreamt of this for decades and yet had no idea anything could produce this level of bliss.

I rock back, then forward no more than an *ince*. The pleasure is so intense I need to pause again to gather control. I rock again, beginning to get the hang of this. I look over to see Axx licking a nipple with his tongue, squeezing the other with his fingers, then kissing her with passion. My Angel is in good hands. All I need to do is focus on the noises she's making. The louder she gets, the longer I'll keep doing what pleases her.

I find a rhythm that pulls a long, low moan from her. I discover an angle that makes her scream louder.

Her hands are clenched in the sheets; I place mine over hers. "I love you, Brianna," I tell her as I increase my pace. She shrieks in pleasure as I feel her muscles clench me stiffly, first her hands, then her tight channel. The experience of her muscles milking me in long, rolling waves is so intense I jet into her as I grunt in satisfaction.

"Oh my God," she says, her breathing still heaving from the exertion and her release. "Wow."

I roll her off Axx and join her on her other side. We're all silent for a moment, well, silent except for our heavy panting.

I want to float in this bliss for just a moment. For just this *minima* I don't want to worry about my gem, but my thoughts flick toward his of their own volition. The fingers of my mind gently reach into his emotions. I sense a modicum of peace. Good.

Brianna

My body feels so good, but after being amped up on hormones all day, I'm not nearly done. Besides, I've been worried about Axx, as well as the whole threesome thing.

First, I just want to enjoy the afterglow. Braxx is curved toward me on one side, stroking my hair and kissing my hand. Axx is kissing me, his hand stroking my thigh as if he knows I'm going to be ready for round two in a moment and he wants to be prepared.

Axx's hand slides higher, tracing the line at the juncture of thigh and torso. If it was softer, it would tickle, but this elicits feelings of a different variety.

"Mmmm," I say as I scoot closer to his touch. He complies by dipping his long, thick finger into me and starting a slow rhythm.

I could find my release in a minute this way, especially now that Braxx's teeth are nipping the tight bud of my breast, but I have other ideas.

I slide out of both of their embrace and crouch between Axx's legs.

"No, Brie," his tone is loud and firm and almost panicked. "Don't!"

I grab his waist and lick downward from his navel. I have a feeling if I don't hurry he's going to heave me off of him, so I slide lower and take him into my mouth in one swift movement. I used to love to do this when we were slaves and the lights were out in our cell block. I learned every movement he liked. I knew the pressure and the pace that drove him wild. His responses then were nothing like they are now.

His cock is still partly flaccid, but I keep my rhythm, licking and swirling and adding vibration with a long, deep moan from the back of my throat. What do you know, he's fully erect, just like the articles on the Intergalactic Database promised.

"I want you both inside me. I want to be fully bondmates," my embarrassed whisper is so soft and low I can't imagine either of them heard me.

But they did.

Axx pulls me up and kisses me with more passion than I've ever felt. "I love you, Brianna. You're a gift." He spears me with a look so long and deep and full of affectionate warmth I feel it to the depths of my soul.

I'm still slick with my arousal as well as Braxx's release. I ease myself down on him in little pulses, reveling in the experience of him filling me, stretching me. I adore this position, being able to look into his eyes. That look I always wanted from him is there now, flowing out of him and into me. The pendant symbolizing our love captures my attention as it swings in and out of my vision.

"Are you sure about this, Angel?" Axx asks. "Braxx can join us another time."

"There's oil on the bedside table," is my reply, even though my voice quavered rather than coming out boldly like I would have preferred.

Braxx applies warm oil to my back hole, tentatively at first. It's arousing as he circles the outer rim. He's taking his time as we both warm to the idea.

Then his finger presses inward in little increments. I'm totally focused on his movements, assessing the feeling.

"That feels good, B," I murmur as I press back into him.

This must give him the permission he was waiting for, because now he's emboldened and moving a bit deeper. I focus on the feeling of tightness, being filled, and the intensity of the experience when a second finger joins the first.

This heightens the pressure, but I can't call it pain in any way. We keep moving, me riding Axx, Braxx moving in me from behind.

"Ready, Angel?" Braxx breathes into my ear.

I'm still a bit nervous, but I answer, "Yes."

He pulls out, slathers himself with oil, and presses against me. What was I thinking? This isn't the size of one finger—or two. These boys are well-endowed. But B goes slow and begins to whisper deliciously dirty things in my ear while Axx urges us both on.

"I'm going to make you come, Brie," Braxx tells me confidently as he presses harder. "I want you to say my name when you do."

He presses a bit stronger as Axx's finger circles my clit. Oh, too many sensations to pay attention to.

Braxx takes that moment to fully breach my backside and the moment of pain comes and goes in an instant.

"Fuck," I moan as I press back toward him. He surges forward and back a few more times until he's fully seated.

"Oh my God. I love you guys," I say. I can't pay attention to anything other than the feeling of being filled by the two males I love more than I've ever loved anything in my lifetime. The combination of emotional as well as physical overwhelm adds to the pleasure.

Braxx is pumping me from the rear, I'm riding Axx, and his hand is doing all the right things to my clit. My noises ramp louder as my release thunders down on me. A moment later I hear Braxx's loud groan from behind me and Axx's short bark from in front.

I collapse on Axx, with Braxx covering me from behind. I can tell he's holding all his weight on his arms so he doesn't squish me, so I tip us all to the side.

"So we're bondmates now?" I smile at Axx.

He spears me with a look so deep, so serious, I'm almost afraid of what he's going to say.

"We've always been bondmates, Brianna. What happened here just spoke to the deepest part of our brains that might not have gotten the message yet."

I smile and press my lips to his. "I think what we just did was eloquent enough to send the message to the buried recesses of my antiquated 'lizard' brain."

"I got the message a long time ago," Braxx says from behind me. "I'm glad you two caught up. I told you everything would work out."

Axxios

I never wanted things to be this way. As a younger male, I envisioned myself hale and hearty when I thought of my first night in my bonding bed. I didn't ask to be paralyzed. If someone had told me this was the way it would be, I would have said it wasn't fair.

But two lunar cycles ago I was a slave bound for death in the gladiator arena, and I thought my gem was dead. If someone had told me then that I'd have the loveliest bondmate in the galaxy laughing and kissing me in my bed within a few lunar cycles, I would have called them a liar.

So no, this isn't exactly what I dreamed of, but it might be more than I deserve. I won't be calling Dr. Mirendi tomorrow. I think I'll be practicing with my exoskeleton, getting back to work on the bridge, and figuring out how to better let my love shine through to my gem and my bondmate.

Chapter Seventeen

Brianna

I woke up this morning feeling well used, and I mean that in a good way. I'm a bondmate! What a terrific twist of fate. I love my guys and they love me.

My heart still breaks for Axx. How terrible such a strong, virile male will never feel anything from the waist down.

I read on the Database that manual stimulation could give him an erection. That worked just like the articles said it would. They also said he could ejaculate, which he did. I hadn't thought that through, though. He orgasmed, but he couldn't fully feel it.

You'd think that would have destroyed him. But he seemed calm and happy last night. And Braxx seemed fine. If Axx was just faking it, Braxx would have picked it up from their twinbond, and I would have picked it up from him.

I feel Braxx stirring on my left. His eyes pop open and the first thing he does is gaze over at me and smile. "Brie looks beautiful with her hair all messed up," he whispers, "the just-*dracked* look becomes you."

I consult my stomach. It's not contracting in discomfort at the "b-word." In fact, I think I just might get used to this.

I feel Axx stir on my right. When I turn my head to say good morning I immediately know something is terribly wrong. His face contracts in worry.

"Axx? What's wrong?"

"My body's numb."

His eyes widen in fright. "Can't move my arms."

"*Drack*!"

B's behind me comming the doctor as he bolts out of bed and pulls on his jumpsuit. I don my clothes in record time, then sit on the chair near Axx's side, my palm pressed to his cheek.

It seems like an eternity until the blue doc comes running in, but I know it's probably been less than two minutes. He's using his medpad to scan Axx, the corners of his mouth tightly drawn down.

"I didn't mention it before," the doctor says, "because I didn't think it was relevant, but my earlier scans indicated that the shrapnel was laced with a previously unknown radioactive isotope. This one hadn't been quantified, but I didn't think it was of any consequence.

"Something is affecting Axxios in an unusual manner, and now I'm wondering if it's due to the unfamiliar qualities of that isotope."

"Cut to the chase, doc," Braxxus orders.

"Axxios's condition should be stable. The fact that his paralysis is spreading has no known cause. Maybe it's the isotope, maybe not. Whatever the reason…" he bites his upper lip and looks down at his pad, avoiding our gaze, "my scans indicate this is unremitting, that it will continue until his muscles cease functioning."

He pauses, then continues in a rush, "even his heart."

"How can you be so certain?" Braxx demands.

"Because in the five *minimas* I've been in this room, the paralysis has spread an additional .05%. This thing is raging through your brother's body."

Silence. Thunderous silence. My heart is pounding in my chest, hot tears pool in my eyes. At first, I'm afraid to look at either of my guys, then I can't tear my gaze away. Axx's jaw is set, his newfound emotions shuttered and tightly locked down. Braxx's sweet face is slack in shock and sadness.

I fist my hands at my sides and try not to cry—Axx doesn't need to be worried about me right this moment.

"So what's the treatment?" I ask forcefully, as if by sheer strength of will I could make Dr. Drayke invent a cure.

"Miss Brianna, I…"

"There is no treatment, Angel," Axx says. Of course, it makes perfect sense that out of all of us he's the strongest, calmest one in the room right now. "I'd put my arms around you if I could."

I climb in next to him and curl up next to his side, one arm slung over him. I press against him tightly and lean up to kiss his golden cheek. He's already fast asleep even though he just woke up.

"What's the timeline, doc?" Braxx asks, his voice breaking as he rubs his hand absentmindedly over his head.

"I've never encountered anything like this before. This is uncharted territory. The scans don't look good, Braxxus. I think he's got days, maybe less. I'm sorry. I'll go to the lab and pour over the Database. I'll have Callista comm all the other ships that were on Fairea that day, see if they have any info. But…"

"Thanks, doc."

It's quiet in the room after Dr. Drayke leaves. Braxx slides into bed on Axx's other side and we just hug each other. Axx is sleeping deeply, at least I hope he's sleeping and not in a coma. I'm crying silently. I reach over Axx and pet Braxx's velvety head.

"This is bad, Brie. *Drack*, my heart is breaking."

"It's like a bad dream. I can't believe this is happening."

"I know this isn't fair to ask, Angel, but can I have an *hoara* alone with him? I wonder if maybe our twinlink..." his voice trails off.

"Absolutely, B. I'll give you time with your gem." I don't feel hurt that he wants time alone with his twin. I've known Axx for two months, they've been intimately connected their entire lives. "I'll bring you food when I come back." I reach over Axx's body, kiss Braxx, and scoot off the bed and out the door.

My feet make their way to the kitchen, although my head is in a complete fog. In every sense of the word, yesterday was my wedding day. Now one of my mates has been given a death sentence. Dear Lord, I just want to stay in this blissful cocoon of numbness. I'd rather not feel anything right now.

I have time on my hands and want to stay busy. I've been meaning to go to the cellblock and visit the geneslave. Yuck, I hate that name—it obviously carries the most vile connotations. It's my fault he's on this ship. Although I've asked the doc how he's doing, I should check on him myself and make sure they're treating him okay.

I visit the kitchen and coax Maddie into making a huge bowl of *sumra*, the noodle porridge all the males seem to love. While she's cooking, I forage in the cold box for leftovers he might like. He was so emaciated, I assume he'll eat whatever I bring.

I snag a huge mound of leftover bake-a-cake and add it to the tray I'm carrying. Thanking Maddie, I wend my way to the belly of the ship.

That's right, Brie, I tell myself, *stay busy, keep moving, help others. Don't think.*

I pause before I get to the cellblock door. Shit, I don't want to enter. I'm filled with a sense of dread. I know what happened in that cell wasn't all bad. Axxios was kind to me and although it was the oddest place in the galaxy to have a sexual awakening, that's what happened here. And I know now this is where I began to fall in love with him. My mate. My mate who's dying.

Stop it, Brie! Keep moving. Step, step, step. Help the geneslave. Don't think.

When I was in this cellblock there was constant fear of being shocked or having my head blown off my shoulders. The Urluts leered at me, I knew they were probably watching us have sex on their hidden cameras. There was continual terror knowing I'd be sold and separated—all that was a true nightmare.

I square my shoulders and kick the door with my heel, hoping whoever's guarding the prisoner will help me in. Stryker's scarred face peers through the window in the metal door and he lets me in, although he doesn't seem happy about it.

"Brianna, I'll take that. You don't have to come in here. I can't imagine you want to revisit the memories you created in this *drackhole*."

"Actually, I came to visit the prisoner."

His eyes narrow and his jaw tightens. "Why?"

"He saved my life. He saved Braxx and Axx's life, Stryker. That's why."

"He's a geneslave. A canine. He's dangerous. I'll take the tray."

I shift out of his reach. "I brought him food and I'd like to talk to him." I can't control my shiver as I offer, "let me have his collar controller and you take a break. I'll be fine." God knows I never want to touch a collar again.

"He's a geneslave, Brianna, and I don't think you'd have the heart to use the collar controller. Let me—"

"You must not know me very well, Stryker. You're not going to talk me out of this. I'm not leaving without giving him his food and talking to him. You might as well take a break." I look him hard in the eyes and square my shoulders.

He gently pulls the tray out of my grip and shoves it through the notch in the bars onto the floor of the cell.

I look at the geneslave for the first time since I walked in. He's in the first cell, maybe eight feet away. His back is pressed into the back corner of his cell and he's studiously avoiding both Stryker and me. I catch him sneaking a quick glance at the heavily-laden tray, then he turns his dead gaze to the floor.

I pull Stryker's chair against the wall in the corridor outside the male's cell. "See? I'll sit here and talk to your prisoner while he eats. Unless he can shimmy through those bars, I'll be as safe as a baby in a crib." I smile up at him sweetly. "Maddie's in the kitchen. Nobody else is there. You two might be able to snag some alone time."

That certainly got his attention. The enticement of sex might have done the trick.

"Here's the collar controller. Promise me you'll use it if you need to." He edges toward the door.

"Absolutely. I'll be fine. I won't leave until you get back."

"Doctore should be here to relieve me in half an *hoara*," he says, and he's out the door at a jog.

I take a moment to glance down the hallway toward the cell where Axx and I were imprisoned. *That's history*, I tell myself as I square my shoulders, *no time to think about that now*.

I notice my fingers fiddling idly with my new necklace, the symbol of our tri-bond. I snatch my hand away as if I'd touched hot coals. I don't need to think of that right now, either.

"Feel free to eat. I'm certainly not going to go in there and fight you for it," I tell the prisoner.

He glances at me, a feral look in his mismatched eyes. He walks on all fours, almost like a dog, to grab the tray, then pulls it to the rear of his cell. With his back toward me, he begins inhaling his food.

I know instinctively that no words will calm him. Nothing I say could soothe him or convince him I won't hurt him, zap his collar, or snatch his food back. Although I have a terrible voice I decide to sing. Of course, the song that flies into my mind is from Brownies about friendship—the one about new friends, silver and gold.

Ah, the power of the subconscious. I wasn't really focusing when that song popped into my mind. A pang of sadness so sharp and so deep threatens to break me, but I push that inside and focus on just this moment.

My terrible singing seems to be working. First, his back straightens a bit; he's not hunched so far over his food. Then he slows down from fast shoveling to normal eating.

Although his back is mostly between me and his food, I can see the plates and his hands. When he moves to eat the cake, I gently tell him, "That's dessert. Most people save that for last." I see him politely set the cake back down and finish everything else.

"You're still way too thin, but it looks like you've put on a bit of weight. I hope they've been feeding you regularly." I figure he's calmed enough I can talk to him instead of continuing to repeat the old song. "I want to apologize for not visiting sooner. I've been preoccupied."

"With your mates?" he asks, his tone deep and gruff.

"How'd you…?" I guess he's smart enough to have picked that up from our behavior during that frantic run on Fairea. "Yes. The gold one was hit by shrapnel, like you."

"But he got sick from it," he offers.

"Yeah, it made him sick and it severed his spinal cord. He's…dying."

Oh my God, did I just say that? Did I just admit that out loud? Tears spring to my eyes, but I tighten my jaw and try to pull myself together.

"Oh. Sorry." He turns a few degrees my way. I can see his profile. I'm not certain he can see me through the shaggy curtain of his snarled hair.

"I'm sorry," I say, trying to pull myself back into the here and now, "I shouldn't have dragged you here. I wanted to save your life. I didn't really think it through, though. I didn't really believe you'd wind up in this cell. I guess I should have left you on Fairea."

"I'd be dead there," his voice sounds so hollow, so resigned.

"So if you could tell me where you want to go, what planet you're from, where your family is, I'll try to convince Zar to take you there. We can get you back where you belong."

"I'm a geneslave."

"I'm new here. I don't understand."

"I was created in a lab. I have no planet other than the one I was created on. I don't even have any acquaintances other than the *drackhole* who tricked me and re-enslaved me, then left me to die in that terrorist attack."

Although his words are sad, his face carries no expression. It's SSDD to him.

"Well...where would you like to go? Certainly you've heard of other places? Somewhere you could be safe, start a new life?"

He shakes his head and turns a few more degrees so we can fully see each other. He reaches for the cake and takes a bit with his fingers—Stryker confiscated the silverware I brought.

When he puts the first bite into his mouth, the expression on his face is comical. It moves in slow motion. The cake enters his mouth and he chews once, then his eyes round, he lets out a short, deep moan from the back of his throat, and instead of inhaling the food, he savors every bite. He slowly chews, as his eyes close in ecstasy. Finally, he swallows with a tiny smile on his face.

He raises his eyebrows at me, needing no words to ask the question.

"Cake," I reply. "It's a treat. That's why you eat it at the end of the meal."

"With food like that, who needs any other?" He takes several minutes eating and savoring every morsel of the cake until there isn't a crumb left on his plate.

"Yeah, I get it. Chocolate cake, chocolate frosting—who could resist?"

"Chocolate," he says it in a hushed tone, like it's a most powerful and beloved deity. Yeah, this BBW can certainly relate.

"I'll bring you some more later. I'll also talk to Zar, the captain, and see if he knows a safe place to take you. I'll try, but I don't know if they'll allow you out of this cell. Everyone seems to fear you."

"Yet you don't. Why?"

"You saved our lives. You carried my mate to safety. You could have run the other way after we cut your bonds. You risked your life for us. Why would I fear you?" He gets quiet and thoughtful.

"Did you think of a name?" I ask.

"Sirius. The Altherian name for a canine."

"Seriously?" Whoops, that probably wasn't nice. "I don't think the canine thing is a compliment. Maybe a name that doesn't call attention to…?"

"It's what I am." It's the most forceful thing I've heard him say.

"Sirius it is, then." I muster a smile. "Pleased to meet you, Sirius." I'm nodding at him, genuinely pleased to call him anything other than "geneslave."

"Pleased to meet you…?"

"Oh, sorry, Brianna."

Doctore's voice interrupts over the comm, "I'll be there in five *minimas*, Stryker."

"I'll come back…at some point…and bring more food—and cake. I'll see if they can get you a shower. I'll talk to Zar about—"

"You've been kind to me Brianna. I will heal your bondmate."

"What?"

"It's one of the reasons I had to run from planet Malego. They bred me to be the perfect fighting machine. I'm stronger than other humanoids twice my size, I have excellent night vision, an animal's sense of smell and hearing, and I have self-healing powers.

"They discovered my blood can be used to heal other species. I'm a geneslave—expendable. They were preparing to drain me completely, kill me to save the life of some rich official. I found a way off-world and took it." His gaze penetrates mine. "I'll heal your mate for you, Brianna," his voice is soft and melodious.

I don't think tears have ever sprung to my eyes like this—my emotions reacted faster than my thoughts could comprehend his words. My feelings are spinning so swiftly I can't think. Is it true? Can he heal Axxios? And, dear God, did he just give me information that he could be killed for? Why would he do that?

"It would work?"

He simply nods.

My mind fast-forwards to my next steps. I imagine telling Zar about Sirius' abilities. I know with certainty he'll say no. He'll insist it's just a trick for Sirius to get out of his cell and break free, that the geneslave is just playing on a heartbroken female's emotions to get his freedom. Zar's had a hard life and isn't very trusting.

The idea that a cure might be sitting less than ten feet from me and Zar would forbid me to take advantage of it tightens my throat. Time is of the essence, I have to figure out how to make this happen, and it has to happen now, right this minute, before Doctore barges through that door.

I come up with the plan in a split second. This will either convince Zar to allow the prisoner out of his cell to heal Axxios, or it will get me killed. I'm willing to die trying to save Axx. The thought shocks me, but I know it's true. I love him so much I'd trade my life for his.

"Sirius, sit with your back to the bars. I'm going to take off your collar."

"Won't this get you in trouble with your shipmates?"

"Hurry!"

He does as I ask. I kneel down, use the collar controller to disable it, and reach between the bars to snatch it off his neck. It's the work of a moment to place it around my own neck and toss the controller into his cell.

Sweat blooms all over my body, an autonomic reaction that bypasses my brain. Part of me wants to tear the fucking thing off and throw it to the end of the hallway, but the rest of me insists I follow through with the plan, however half-baked it is.

Sirius backs away from the device, his hands up, palms toward me. "What are you doing Brianna?" his voice is a shocked whisper.

"When Doctore gets here you can threaten to kill me if they don't release you. You'll have all the power. You can get out of that cell and make them take you to a safe planet."

He kicks the controller toward me, then retreats until his back is against the rear of the cell. "No! I don't want to hurt you. I don't want to hurt anyone!"

"Use me, take me as a hostage. You deserve a life. But will you help my mate first?" I shove the controller toward him again.

"What the *drack*?" Doctore has walked into the cellblock, assessed the scene, and is aiming his laser weapon at Sirius as I scream, "NO!" and rush to stand between the two males, my arms outstretched. "Don't hurt him, Doctore, this is my fault."

The gladiator still has his weapon in his two outstretched hands, pointed at Sirius. "Step away, Brianna. How did this cur manage to collar you?"

"I collared myself. Stand down. I did this to help him escape, but he wants no part in it and I'm afraid you're going to kill him due to my stupidity."

I glance behind me and see Sirius facing the rear, his palms against the wall.

Doctore slowly lowers his gun, and I heave a sigh of relief. I've never acted so impulsively, or done something so foolish in all my life.

~.~

An hour later I'm in our cabin with my two bondmates, the doctor, and Captain Zar, trying to explain my reckless behavior. "It seemed like a good idea at the time...I knew I had to act fast. I just thought you'd never let him out of his cell, Zar. I wanted him to get a chance to help Axx if he could."

"You could have gotten yourself killed Brianna," Zar scolds. "Doctore could have shot the geneslave, who sounds innocent of all wrongdoing." He shakes his leonine head, his lips pressed into a flat line as he spears me with a disappointed look.

"The decision about the procedure is yours, Axx," Zar's tone is now calm and supportive.

"I spoke with the geneslave, who's eager to cooperate," says Dr. Drayke. "I consider myself a good judge of character and I can't discern any motive other than a sincere desire to help. He knows he'll be tied to the gurney and there will be a contingent of gladiators at the ready if he makes any moves. It sounds as if it's not much more complicated than a simple transfusion."

"You say I've got a day or two at most doc?" Axx asks, his voice level.

Drayke nods solemnly.

"Sounds like I have very little to lose."

Axxios

An *houra* later Sirius and I were stretchered into medbay,
two *houras* after that the transfusion was complete. This was
the least invasive procedure I've endured since my injury.
Sirius was kind and respectful throughout.

The tiny medbay exam area didn't have room for anyone
other than Sirius and me on our stretchers, Braxx and
Doctore who were heavily armed in case the geneslave
made any moves to harm anyone, and Dr. Drayke. I felt bad
that Brie was relegated to wait in the hallway, but the
procedure didn't take long.

Whatever the ultimate outcome of the transfusion, I realize
Sirius risked his life to save mine.

"I don't know why you offered to save my life, Sirius, but
you're smart enough to know the information you entrusted
us with could get you killed. I'll never be able to repay you.
Whether this procedure works or not, know that I'm indebted
to you."

"It was the right thing to do. I wish you well," is his reply. I
vow to myself that I'll never call him a geneslave again.

Neither Sirius nor Dr. Drayke knew how long it would take for
me to see results, if there were any.

As they stretcher me back to our room, I consider giving
Brianna the wrath of seven hells for pulling that stunt in the
cellblock. When I think of her delicate neck surrounded by
that *dracking* collar I want to break things.

Back in our cabin, Braxx laid me on the middle of the bed, and now I have my silver twin on one side and Brianna on the other.

It's my life's biggest irony that I've found my bondmate and regained my link with both my gem and my emotions within days of receiving a death sentence. I worry about Brie and Braxx, wondering how they'll do without me.

I have no faith in this procedure working, I thought it would distract Brie through the next couple days. It will give her something to hope for and keep her from mourning me before I'm gone.

Brie

The last two days have been steeped in heartache and finality. Axx has been sleeping twenty-three hours a day, turning his head fitfully and making pained noises. He's been paralyzed from the neck down since this morning.

When he's awake he's been a joy to be with, which makes the situation more poignant, if that's even possible. The taciturn, isolative male I initially met is gone. He's now a complete person willing to talk about his emotions and connect with his gem and me.

Every time he wakes up he apologizes for hurting my feelings when he was still his emotionless gold self. I've told him to stop saying such things, I forgave him days ago.

He admits he's loved me since he was five, just like his gem. This pains my heart even more.

He's so thoughtful, he made B and me promise to take care of Sirius. Although it's not the first thing on my mind, I plan on talking to Captain Zar about releasing him from the cellblock.

Axx and Braxx have had a few brief, private conversations. Braxx tearfully told me they've already said their goodbyes.

I know I should talk to Axx—give us both closure—but I haven't been able to force myself to do so. I'm not sure I've avoided it because I still believe the transfusion will miraculously work, or simply because I'm the galaxy's biggest coward and I just don't want to say my heartbreaking goodbyes to one of the males I love.

Dr. Drayke stops by to perform scans three or four times a day, and although the progression of the paralysis has slowed, it hasn't stopped. We all know it's a matter of hours before his heart stops beating.

We're lying in bed in a sandwich. Ever since the transfusion, Axx has been the peanut butter, and B and I have been the bread. Axx is out of it, it's a state deeper than sleep. I lift my head and see that Braxx is awake. I reach over and rub his spiky hair, I know he likes that. "How you doing, B?"

"Sad, Brie. Not much time, listen to his breathing."

I've been trying not to acknowledge it, but I noticed that his labored breathing of a few hours ago is softer and slower now.

"Can you feel him through your twinlink?"

"For the last few days it's flickered from nothing when he's out of it, to pain when he's awake." He sighs.

Axx's breathing quickens and his eyes pop open. With all the pain he's in, it's sweet and surprising that the first thing he does when he awakens is smile at me, then his gem.

"Beautiful Brianna," he says sweetly as he reaches out to sweep my hair off my face.

"Axx?" I say. He hasn't been able to move his arms in over thirty-six hours.

"Gods!" he declares as he moves his hands to pat his thighs and calves.

I watch under the covers as he moves his legs, then wiggles his toes. "Look!" he announces as he throws the blankets off and bends his knees.

I thought we were sharing the last hours of his life, and here he is fully functional. My face is stretched into a wide smile—I've never felt happiness like I do this minute. I want to cry and laugh at the same time. My head is spinning. Part of me is too afraid to believe this could be happening, and the other wants to believe it with all my heart and soul.

I've known I've loved Axx for days, but now, with his strong arms around both Braxx and me in the tightest hug, my chest is so full and warm I feel I'll burst.

He looks at me with all the love in the universe. His features are soft, full of warmth, and focused fully on me.

Yes, this is the look I've always wanted, and it seems I'll never lack for it again. It comes easily to Axx now, and he doesn't seem shy about sharing it.

"I have the best gem and the most beautiful bondmate in the galaxy," Axx pronounces, never taking his eyes off mine.

"All in agreement, say yes," Braxx says jubilantly.

"Yes!" we all shout.

"We all agree with that," Axx says with a smile, "but are you ready for a lifetime of being outvoted, Brie?"

"Yes if it means we get to stay bondmates," I nod happily. I look down and notice that *everything* below his waist is working perfectly. I stifle the urge to test out its full functionality—that can wait. Right now I sink next to him, nestle my head on his bicep and throw my arm around both him and as much of Braxx as I can reach. I feel Braxx's arm stroke my back as he pulls me in even tighter.

I know we'll be testing Axx's stamina in this bed in a few hours, but right now all I want to do is bask in how fabulous I feel right now.

That weird energy exchange like we experienced on Fairea is happening. A loop of strong energy circling and whirling from one to the other.

It builds with every circuit, enveloping us. It's so thick and so real it almost feels like I could reach out and touch it. It's as if our molecules are mixing and blending with each other: Axx's into me, mine into Braxx, all of it circling and mingling and decimating any barriers that remain between the three of us.

I'll forever be part of these guys, and they're now part of me. This is the tri-bond—I don't need to know it's complete. And it's real, as authentic and strong as hardened steel.

I don't even know how to describe it. It's more than the deepest love. I feel more full than a cup that's overflowing. I'm complete in every way. And safe. I'm so safe in their loving arms.

I open my eyes and look at them. I feel such a tremendous overwhelm—a rush of love and acceptance flowing from me to them, then doubling, tripling, and hurtling back to me again.

"It will be like this forever?" I'm almost breathless.

"Yes," they both respond at once. They're smiling. It's so wonderful, such a relief to see a wide, happy grin on Axx's face especially. He's changed, that's obvious. I imagine he's thrilled to be released from the prison of his constrained emotions. Now he's free to receive and express love.

My face is stretched tight in a broad smile. I have my beautiful silver and gold bondmates. I'm snuggled in a big bed on a swift ship full of friends who love me. I don't know where we're going, or if we'll ever find a place to settle down. Frankly, I don't care. What I have, right here, right now, is so much more than I ever hoped for.

"I love you guys," I tell them.

"We love you, too," they both reply.

"If there are Gods, I'm blessed. You two are truly a gift," Axx says, hugging us both and kissing me. "If we weathered this, we can get through anything."

"I told you it would all work out," Braxx says. "It always does."

Epilogue
One lunar cycle later

Brianna

Life onboard the *Lazy Slacker* can be harrowing, so we'll use any excuse to have a party. Tonight's excuse can be blamed on me—I've organized a game of charades. Yeah, I can see the folly of my plan, none of these big aliens know a thing about Earth's pop culture references. But then again, none of us Earth women know the names of the two thousand gladiator drinking songs these guys have a penchant for singing at any given opportunity. I guess we're even.

I realize I'm absentmindedly fondling the pendant that hangs between my breasts. I haven't removed it since Axx placed it over my head a month ago. It symbolizes every wonderful thing about my life, and right now, there are so many wonderful things I can barely track them.

Dax made me a massage table. You'd think his huge fingers would be clumsy, but he's the handiest male I've ever met. I've set up shop in the *ludus*, giving massages to anyone who asks. I enjoy feeling like I'm a productive part of our big family.

Speaking of our big family, just about everyone is here in the dining room, cleaning up after the amazing dinner Maddie made. Tonight was Vren cordon bleu with pearled hespers— delish.

The guys are moving tables and setting up for us to break into two groups for our game of charades. Shadow's picking up a long table single-handedly, showing off his muscles for Petra, although I don't know why. The way she looks at him, like he hung the moon, leaves no doubt that she's crazy-in-love with him.

Blue Dr. Drayke and Nova have finally gotten to the point where they can leave their room and keep their hands off each other for hours at a time. Although you'd never know it by looking at them now. Nova's on his lap, and he's feeding her the last bites of dinner. I understand they have a mindlink, and by the looks of it he just shared something so filthy with her she's blushing a deep shade of crimson.

Sirius is seldom seen in the company of more than one person at a time, and usually he's got his back safely against a wall. However tonight the siren song of chocolate cake has lured him away from the edges of the room. To look at him you'd never know how emaciated he was only a month ago. Whatever the Feds did to his genes, he definitely looks strong and healthy now.

Axx and Braxx convinced Zar to give him a cabin instead of a cell. They've kind of adopted him. My guys coaxed him to eat with us a few times, and it's been surprising to get to know him. I believe he's the smartest being I've ever met. And kind. I don't know how someone who's been beaten and abused his whole life can be so full of compassion. All I know is he saved Axx's life, and for that, I'll always be in his debt.

Zar's got his ubiquitous pad with him, he probably has a few announcements he wants to share. Raised a slave all his life, he takes everything very seriously, which is good because he's in charge of keeping us all alive. I love watching him and his "beloved Anya" as he calls her. They look at each other the way I always yearned for.

And speaking of yearning, here come my guys. They left after dinner and I wondered if there was a surprise in store for me. They must have gone to our room to change, because look at them, striding in wearing their sexy black leather gladiator togs.

Honestly, I don't know why they bother, they don't have to try to impress me. They could be wearing rags and I'd still want to jump their bones.

"Hey handsomes," I say as I hurry to greet them. "You guys look terrific."

"And you look beautiful as always, Brie," Axx tells me, his eyes openly full of love.

"Your flattery is great, but don't think for a minute you're going to escape your punishment," Braxx scolds me.

"But I didn't earn any punishments today," I protest.

"Don't worry, we'll think of something." Braxx winks at me with a lascivious grin.

"I can't wait," I say with a smile, although we've got all the time in the galaxy.

The End

Dear Reader,

I hope you enjoyed reading <u>Axxios and Braxxus</u> as much as I loved writing it. I'm sure you're wondering about intriguing Sirius the dog-man. Is he going to get his own book? Heck yes!

Sirius will be the next book in the Galaxy Gladiator series. How could you not love this guy? His character arc of growth and change is going to be sexy, exciting, and totally unexpected. The first chapter of his book isn't quite ready for prime time, but I'll be posting it soon in my <u>Free Newsletter</u>—so sign up <u>here</u>.

If you read book Four in the Galaxy Gladiators Series, <u>Devolose</u>, you might be wondering if you'll see more of the hunky pirates. I've enclosed a **SNEAK PEEK** for you, it will be the first book in the Galaxy Pirates spinoff series: <u>Sextus</u>. With a name like that how could anything go wrong?

I'm planning a lot of new content and giveaways in my free newsletter, so here's the link to sign up. The free content right now is a complete novelette of Shadow's tragic and sexy backstory: <u>Terminus.</u>

FREE NEWSLETTER SIGNUP
www.alanakhan.com/free-copy/

Request for Reviews: Reviews equal love for an author, and also help us keep writing. You don't need to write a book report unless you want to, just a few sentences about how my book made you feel, and what you liked (or didn't). I promise I read every single one. Here's a link to make leaving a review even easier.

Leave a review on Amazon for Axxios and Braxxus.

Hugs,

Alana

Follow me on Facebook at Alana Khan Author and Khan's Tribe

Follow me on Twitter at alanakhanauthor

Galaxy Pirates
Book One
Sextus

Chapter One

Lexa

"I found the coordinates to your Earth." Sextus's lips quirk smugly as he straddles the chair next to me in the small dining area of our vessel. He's tall and muscular, the largest of the seven huge alien males on board this small pirate spaceship. I'm certain it's no accident he caught me in here alone.

"Oh, thank God. When can Captain Thantose get us there?" Relief floods every cell in my body. I feel my muscles relax even though Sextus is sitting far too close—he's so big and tough, not to mention blue with tribal markings, I usually do my best to avoid him.

"Our ship is carrying a load of exotic Primian fish bound for Algaron IV. Seven days to that planet to offload and then twelve days back to Earth."

"That's nineteen days! How will I explain my absence if I'm gone from Earth that long? I'll talk to Thantose." I stand, ready to hustle to the bridge and plead my case to the captain. "I'm sure he can drop me on Earth, then deliver his cargo later."

"Those fish are delicate. We're losing four percent of them a day. That's expensive merchandise; we can't afford that big a loss."

Why is he looking at me like the cat that's about to eat the canary?

"I'm certain he'll see the light." I turn to leave.

"I already informed him. He said Earth would have to wait."

His savage gaze flicks to my chair as if he's commanding me to take a seat. I silently curse my cowardice as I follow his unspoken order to sit.

"I take it you have some reason you're personally delivering this news...other than to gloat." My eyes narrow, I think I know what's coming next.

"I paid good credits to my cousin, who works for the MarZan cartel. He risked life and limb to get me the coordinates to your Earth. We stop on planet Neron first thing tomorrow to refuel.

"I located a small ship we can rent. It can not only get us to Earth in five days but has the ability to put you down anywhere you designate with its state-of-the-art matter transporter. I didn't put a hold on it, I was waiting for your approval before I spend half an *annum's* pay to rent the rig."

His stare is positively feral. I figure this is the moment I'm supposed to plead for more information, but as desperate as I am to get back home, I'll never stoop to begging.

"What's your ask?" I spear him with a feral look of my own. I don't think I need my Ph.D. in psychology to know the nature of what he wants. His lusty glances haven't been subtle since the day he and the rest of the crew rescued us from certain death where I was imprisoned on planet Paradise with two other Earth women—we were all bound for sexual slavery.

He grabs a grape-like fruit from a bowl in the center of the dining table and pops it into his mouth. "The cost?" He cocks an eyebrow. "You provide whatever service I request on the trip from Neron to your planet." He chews nonchalantly as he cocks his head to one side. He seems to be savoring my discomfort more than his bite of food.

"Fuck you, Sextus." He had to know I'd never agree to that proposition.

I rise to leave, but before I'm through the doorway he says, "Do the math, little Lexa." I pause, my back still to him. "You were in a cell for ten days on planet Paradise, eight days since we rescued you and your friends. Five days to Earth if we leave tomorrow from Neron. That's twenty-three days if you come with me. Thirty-seven if you stay on this ship.

"I don't know *drack* about Earth, but I wonder just how long you can be gone from a place before your explanation about your absence becomes suspicious.

"The other females have already said they've been gone too long. They know they can't go back, they...what was it they said? They would be locked up by your military and studied? I don't think you have the luxury of fourteen extra days to go all the way to Algaron IV and back. I believe I'm your ticket home, little Lexa, and I just set the price."

"Just because you're an asshole, Sextus, doesn't mean I'm a whore." I stalk through the door, but before I move out of earshot I hear, "Not just sexual services, I was hoping you know how to cook. My offer stands until 2400." His amused laugh follows me as I run down the short hallway to the room I share with Carrie, one of the two Earth females I was rescued with.

Luckily she isn't here. I throw myself on my bed and try to think. My hands are shaking with rage. I let out a low scream from the back of my throat and kick my legs in frustration.

"Fuck, fuck, fuck." I pound the bed with each expletive. "Okay, Lexa, try to think." I leap to a standing position and pace in tight circles.

Before I can problem solve, my mind chooses this moment to throw me a quick reminder of the last three miserable weeks of my life. I was abducted from Earth then placed in a cell with Carrie and Brin, who were kidnapped years ago. We were all rescued by seven huge alien pirates whose looks scare the shit out of me, then taken to planet Primus for a week with the offer to start a new life there.

Brin stayed on Primus to recover from the trauma of a long captivity. Carrie chose to stay on this ship to look for a new life on a different planet. And me? I'm still hoping I can find my way back to Earth.

All the alien males except for Sextus have been super nice and have tried very hard to get us back home, But until today, no one knew the coordinates of Earth except for the MarZan cartel which apparently uses our planet to harvest free breeding females whenever they choose.

I've been aware for days that if I don't get back to Earth soon, I won't be able to return at all. How many weeks can I claim to have been in some fugue state with no memory of where I've been and what I've been doing? I've concocted a story about walking the Appalachian Trail and getting lost, but my plausible deniability is about to expire.

Sextus is right. I don't have an extra fourteen days to get home. If I wait much longer, when I do get back to Earth the special forces guys will arrive in their black helicopters to fly me to Area 51 for some anal probing of their own.

"Four days!" I shout to the empty room. I was four days from getting my Ph.D. in Psychology. In order to get my degree at twenty-three, I've had to put my entire life on hold for the past seven years.

I was home-schooled and earned my high school diploma at sixteen. After my dad died, I enrolled in college and didn't take a break for the next seven years. I never had a summer off, took the maximum amount of credits every semester, and just plowed through to get my degree. No friends, no family, no lovers, just nose to the grindstone all with one goal—the degree.

Now my life is completely derailed.

There is no future for me in space—absolutely none.

Several hours later, Carrie asks if I want dinner, but I have no appetite. I just watch the clock, waiting for the midnight deadline. No matter how you cut it, my dilemma boils down to two choices: never go home again, or be Sextus' sex slave for five days.

The choice seems obvious when I put it like that. I've worked my ass off for the last seven years to get to my goal—to become a psychologist. Am I willing to throw all that away because the cost of five days of embarrassment is too high?

No. I've known for hours I was going to do it. I just wasn't ready to admit it to myself.

It's ten to midnight. Carrie's been sleeping on the top bunk for hours. I need to quit procrastinating and do the walk of shame to Sextus's room.

Luckily the hallway's deserted and he's only four doors down. His electronic sliding door is cracked an inch. He left it open for me, the fucker. He knew I'd come.

I knock lightly until I hear his deep, "Come in."

The lights are dim, so it takes me a moment to fully absorb the scene in front of me. Sextus is on the bed, head leaned against the back wall, covers only pulled up to his thighs. His muscled blue body with its swirling cobalt tribal markings is in stark contrast to the white sheets. His meaty blue hand is slowly fisting his penis from base to tip as he spears me with an animalistic gaze.

"You're here with four *minimas* to spare. Nicely played, little Lexa." He flashes a smile as his hand continues its leisurely journey, stroking up and down.

Okay, Lexa, I order myself, *you will not close your eyes. You will not look away. You will not blush.* I calculated it out, five days is 7,200 minutes. I can do that standing on my head. I will do what needs to be done so I can have the life I've been planning—the life I deserve.

"I need to hear it, Lexa. Why are you here?"

I forbid myself to pause or stammer. "I'm here to accept your proposal." I stare straight at him, my gaze never wavering. My voice sounded steady, that's good. It's so dim in here I doubt he can see my carotid artery rapidly leaping in my throat.

"Good. I knew the day I met you that we were two of a kind, you and I."

What would possibly make this monster think such a thing? I'm not asking.

"I've watched you with the other females, you don't care about hurting anyone's feelings. Neither do I. Seems like both of us follow the philosophy: take care of yourself and damn everyone else. We'll do fine for the next five days."

I turn to leave.

"Where do you think you're going?" his voice is harsh and low, almost a growl.

I don't respond. I know it isn't really a question. He and my dad must have gone to Power and Control University together.

"You need to hear the terms of service and agree to them, little Lexa."

I stand straighter, tighten my jaw, and look him square in the eye. Does he think this little Earth female has never been afraid before? Fuck him. I learned how to deal with this kind of psychological torment at my daddy's knee.

"One. You'll tell no one the terms of our contract or I will not fulfill them. Even if you don't fully trust me, I have every intention of delivering you to your home planet—on time. I have gone to considerable expense to obtain the coordinates and the fastest ship available. I'm a total *dracker*, but I am a male of my word. When I return to this ship without you, I have to live with all these people and I'd prefer our contract to be just between us. Is that clear?"

I nod.

"Say it."

"Yes, that's clear."

"You can call me sir."

Fuck. "Yes, sir." Is this going to be some <u>Fifty Shades of Grey</u> bullshit?

"Two. You will do exactly as I say or you will be punished."

Okay. I guess that's a "yes" on the <u>Fifty Shades</u> question.

"Is that clear?"

"Yes, sir." I try to put as much "fuck you" as I can into the "sir."

"Three. My cousin is a congenial male who told me Earth's coordinates for free. Reserving the vessel, however, will require a significant amount of credits. Since I am acting in good faith, I will need a clear gesture on your part that you are acting in good faith as well. Strip out of your clothes." He gives me a self-satisfied smile. "Computer, turn lights up."

I'm an idiot. How is it that a savvy individual like myself did not anticipate this particular level of hell? I don't hesitate, though, I've decided to do this and I will follow through.

I swiftly pull off my t-shirt, leggings, bra, and panties. I knew I'd need to do it quickly in order to get it done. I also didn't want it to appear sensual in any way. I order my sympathetic nervous system not to blush. I will get through this. I toss my head and hope I give the appearance of supreme indifference even though my hands are shaking and my pulse is pounding.

Although I'm looking him directly in the eye, my peripheral vision catches his fingers tightening around his cock.

"Are we done? May I leave?" My clothes are still balled in my hands. I'm about to turn toward the door, planning to get dressed and run to the safety of my room.

"No."

I don't recall ever hearing this particular timbre of deep growl escape a male's throat before. I'm paralyzed in fear, but hope I seem stubborn and confident.

"Let's review the rules one more time. What is rule number two?"

"Do as you say," I answer without hesitation.

"Put your clothes on the foot of the bed."

I toss them there.

"You're trying my patience, little Lexa. I guess we'll have fun on the trip to Earth as I teach you how to follow the rules." This is more of a promise than a threat. "One final thing before you leave." He sits up, hangs his legs over the side of the bed and beckons me between his knees. "To ensure you don't change your mind after I pay for the vessel, I want proof of how serious you are about abiding by the contract."

He pauses, then, "Suck my cock," his voice is rough and breathy.

I'm certain he has to see my jaw lock tight and the blood drain from my face. Crap.

I guess my being a virgin shouldn't be a big deal. Really, I should have done something about it years ago. I was just far too busy studying my ass off and writing my doctoral fucking dissertation.

Okay, Lexa, you can do this. How hard can it be? What was it they said in Victorian days? Close your eyes and think of England? Whatever. I focus on the fact that this is my choice. I could tell him to forget this ridiculous contract and then run out of the room. But I'm not going to do that. Because I want to get back to my life on Earth and this is my only escape.

I'm going to do this, and I'm going to do this in style. I pull myself to my full five-foot-two inches and act like there's a crown on my head. I'm a queen and I relinquish my power to no man.

My knees hit the floor between his feet and I try to get my bearings. I've seen plenty of cocks before; just because I'm a virgin doesn't mean I haven't stumbled onto Porn Hub. Of course, I've never seen one this long or this thick before. Nor have I ever seen one that is two shades of blue.

I form my plan of attack. *Swift, sure, no time for hesitation, Lexa, just go for it.* I grab him at the root, press my mouth over the head, and engulf him as far down as I can go in one swift movement because I don't want to hesitate or gag.

"*Drack!*" he thunders as he grabs my shoulders and pulls me up and off of him. "What the *drack* female? If you didn't want to go through with the contract why did you come to my room?"

I'm standing, staring at him, just blinking. "What?" I ask, then hastily add, "sir?"

"Teeth! Seven hells, female. You used your teeth!" Even in the dim light, I can see the whites all around his irises, his eyes wide in surprise.

"I...didn't know."

"What are you saying? Are human cocks impervious to pain?"

"I don't know...I've never..."

"You're untouched?" He pulls back, nostrils flared, muscles rigid.

Ohhh, the way he's saying that, like it's the worst thing in the known galaxy, I don't want to cop to that. So I just stand here, wondering if I drew blood.

"Answer me. You've never...been with a male?"

"No." He's still staring daggers through me. "Sir."

"Why in the galaxy did you accept my offer, Lexa? I thought we were like-minded. I thought this would be a game for both of us, that I'd be the aggressor and you'd feign innocence. I had no idea you *were* an innocent." He stands, grabs my clothes from the foot of the bed, and gently hands them to me. "I rescind my offer. The contract is null and void."

Sextus

"No. Please. Sextus, I'll...do better next time."

Her voice is pleading, but by her pinched face and downturned mouth, this is costing her every iota of her dignity.

I'm a *drackhole*. I've always been one. I'm used to getting my way. But not this.

"I need to get back to Earth. Teach me how to do...that..." She glances at my cock, now tucked against my body, shriveled in pain. "Teach me and I'll do it."

I don't want to prolong this one moment longer. I don't want her to give away every shred of her self-respect.

"Go back to your room, Lexa. I don't understand Earth ways. I can't play my games with an untouched." I stalk to my restroom. "When I come out I want you gone."

Glossary

Ahnseek angel—guardian angel
BBW—Big Beautiful Woman
Cestus match—an ancient type of gladiatorial combat not fought to the death. Fought in the nude.
drack—the perfect all-purpose expletive. It's a noun, it's a verb, it's an adjective.
Fairea (Fair-ee-uh)
FFS—For fuck's sake
SSDD—Same Shit Different Day
Swipe Left—a term from a dating application where you swipe right if interested, swipe left if not

Who's Who

Initially paired in cells together by their captors:

Dahlia and Dax (almost seven feet tall, described as looking like a Neanderthal)
Grace and Shadow (prosthetic left eye and arm)
     Shadow's now with Petra
     Grace is with Tyree who was little & sexless until his recent transformation
Anya and Zar (feline humanoid with mane and tail)
Zoey and Steele (silver skin)
Savannah and Theos (Norse-god looking with white hair and light skin)
Maddie and Stryker (scarred face)
Brianna and Axxios (gold skin)
Callista and Aries
Heather and Savage
Rileigh and Doctore (trainer in the *ludus*, ebony skin, which is pebbled on shoulder and pec)

Nova and Dr. Drayke sun Omrun are now mated (he has blue skin)

Copyright

Axxios and Braxxus: Book Six in the Galaxy Gladiators
Series (BBW/Mengage) by Alana Khan

P.O. Box 18393, Golden, Co 80402

www.alanakhan.com

© 2019 Alana Kahn

Cover by Elle Arden